SWITCH HITTER

USA TODAY BESTSELLING AUTHOR

SARA NEY

Switch Hitter
A Jock Hard Novella
Copyright © 2017 by Sara Ney
Cover Design by Okay Creations
Formatting by Uplifting Designs

Copyright © 2018 by Sara Ney

ISBN: 978-0-9990253-8-3

First Edition: January 2018

For more information about Sara Ney and her books, visit:
www.authorsaraney.com

SWITCH HITTER

USA TODAY BESTSELLING AUTHOR
SARA NEY

CHAPTER ONE

AMELIA

"I need you to pretend to be me next weekend."

I stop eating, fork poised above my plate. "Why?"

"I have two dates on the same night—oops." My twin sister says it in a *duh* tone of voice, like it should have been obvious.

"No."

"Please? Come on! It'll be fun."

"No." I ignore the whining tone in her voice, the one that rises a few decibels every time she speaks. "Pretending to be someone else isn't fun for me—it's stressful."

"You're no fun."

I laugh. "Exactly my point. If I had to spend an entire night faking it, I would pass out from exhaustion."

"Maybe, but Dash is so hot, you won't even care."

"Is that supposed to be a selling point? This guy you're dating is hot?" I shove lettuce in my mouth and chew. Swallow. "Lucy, we look *nothing* alike."

Okay, so that's not *exactly* true. We're almost identical, I just hate admitting it.

"He doesn't know I'm a twin. Trust me, he won't notice."

This gives me pause. "How does he not know you're a twin?"

"I mean, it's not like we sit and *talk* about you," she quips.

"Right, but don't you tell him about yourself? Normally you love to talk, and the twin thing is kind of a fun fact." And a huge part of *who you are as a human being*, I want to add, but instead, I clamp my lips shut.

"Of course I tell him about myself. I tell him my favorite foods so if he ever decides to take me to dinner he'll know what I like, and I tell him my favorite movies so he's prepared in the event that we go to one. I also show him my best side when I'm taking selfies."

How are we related?

She twirls her hair. "But we've only gone out like, twice—I don't count seeing him at house parties and stuff. He's kind of annoying though, always trying to have deep, meaningful discussions."

My face contorts. "Why would you have a problem with that?"

"Oh my God, Amelia, it's not like we can have a serious talk in the middle of a party."

"What did you say his name was?"

"Dash Amado."

I chuckle into my espresso. "Luce, I hate sounding like an ass, but how deep a discussion could a guy named *Dash* possibly want to have?"

"That's kind of a bitchy thing to say. You don't even know him." She blows out a puff of air. "Besides, I don't think that's his real name."

I slurp my water to annoy her.

It works.

"How about you try harder to get to know him?"

"I'm trying, but you won't help me!"

"Far be it from me to judge, but methinks you're not trying hard *enough*. Stop trying to make me your stand-in."

"For the tenth time, he won't even know it's you."

"I am *not* going on this date for you! It was cute trading places in high school, but it's not cute now." Not to mention, it's immature.

"You used to think it was fun."

"Remember the time we both ran for student council? It was exhausting and embarrassing and the whole mess was completely your fault."

"What are you even talking about? The whole thing was not a mess—everything turned out great! We both got elected."

When we were freshmen in high school, Lucy and I were both running for class officer—president for her, vice president for me. The election speeches were during an assembly during the school day, but rather than showing up, Lucy spent the entire period making out with some football player in a supply closet they'd found unlocked en route to the gymnasium.

In a panic—because I was always so freaking *responsible*—I tried covering for her. Pulled a speech out of my ass, gave it in front of the entire student body, then borrowed a shirt from our friend Clarissa, changed, came back as me to give a speech for myself.

It was exhausting, and the entire time, she was shut in a closet kissing some boy.

My sister gives me a dull look over the rim of her glass, waving her hand in the air dismissively.

"Amelia, that happened five years ago, or whatever the math is. Why do you keep bringing it up? We were in high school."

"I keep bringing it up because I was terrified we were going to get caught! Just like I am now!"

"You're so dramatic. We both won, so I don't know what your problem is."

"The problem is, you're always doing this. Remember that time I dressed up as you to meet Kevin Richards at the movies so you could go do *God knows what* with Dusty Sanders? The entire movie Kevin kept trying to put his hand on my thigh because you'd let him get to third base the night before."

"And you whacked him in the balls," she deadpans dryly. "Yeah, who could forget that?"

"Whatever," I mumble. "He had it coming."

"Can we focus on Dash here, please?"

"We are twenty-one years old—don't you think we're a little old to be pulling tricks on people?"

"Um, no? There's a *reason* God gave us the same face."

That makes me laugh. "You're ridiculous."

"But you love me, don't you?" She bats her sooty lashes. "You're totally going to help me out—I can tell by the look on your face."

"What look?" I pretend I don't know what she's talking about. "I have a look?"

My sister claps her hands, excited. "Yes, you totally do, and you're totally doing this for me!" She lifts her brows and quirks the corner of her mouth into a cocky grin that mirrors the one I have on my face right now.

Shit. She's right.

My twin leans in, hands folded on the table like she's just entered negotiations in a business meeting.

"What's it going to take for you to help me out?"

I mimic her pose. "I don't know, Lucy. You tell me—what's my time worth to you?"

She stares for a few long moments, lost in thought, trying to measure my sincerity through narrowed eyes. She's trying to gauge if I'm being flippant or sincere about helping her. The thing about my sister is that everything always come so easy for her. She's beautiful and relies heavily on her looks, uses them to her advantage. She's outgoing and uses that, too.

Not that I'm not—I'm all of those things, but I'm not a *user*.

My sister is.

She doesn't do it on purpose; she just…wants what she wants, when she wants it.

Lucy isn't mean or malicious, goodness no, nor has she ever stood in the way of me being happy. She's never pulled any deviant twin crap or made me feel bad about our differences.

She's just…Lucy.

When I continue eating my salad and ignoring her hard stares, she sighs loudly, resigned. Pushes a carrot around its plastic container and sighs again.

Drama is my twin sister's middle name.

Her hair is too big, her lips are too red, and her personality is too wild.

Around campus, in certain circles, we're called the Barbie twins. It's not because we have blonde hair—which we don't—but because of Lucy's bombshell appearance. We're tall and slender with thick, wavy hair. My sister has hers shorter by a few inches, layered around her face, and it's a rich chestnut color. Mine is longer and darker.

"What's your time worth to me? I'll buy you an extra gift at Christmas—"

"Which Mom and Dad will pay for."

She sighs at me a third time, this one ending with a little drawn-out groan.

I throw her a bone, rolling my eyes. "So what's up with this guy—what does a *Dash* person do?"

This opening perks her up considerably, and she immediately sits up in her seat, enthusiastic. "He's on the baseball team—the *catcher.*"

"The catcher, ooh la la! Exciting." I'm such a sarcastic jerk sometimes. "And why are you saying the word catcher like that, all whispery?" My head gives a shake. "Am I supposed to be impressed?"

I bet he's the captain or something cliché. Lucy only dates the most handsome, popular guys she can sink her long, manicured claws into. These days, those claws are painted hot pink, and when she's impatient, she taps them on the laminate tabletop to irritate me—like she's doing now.

"Let me guess"—I smirk—"they call him Dash because he's soooo so super fast."

Her smile fades. "You're a smartass, do you know that? But also, you're correct."

"What else does he do quickly?" I joke.

"I don't know." She chomps down on her vegetables. "We've only made out once, but I'm hoping to find out soon. He's giving me blue balls."

"What do you mean you've only made out once? He's a flipping *baseball* player. Forgive me for sounding confused or for buying into stereotypes, but aren't most athletes major horn dogs?"

"Dash isn't like all those guys, Amelia. He's a gentleman, and honestly, it's kind of getting annoying."

I thought the point of her dating these guys was to be seen with them, not to form emotional attachments and actually spend quality time with them.

"It's just frustrating. I'm trying to change his mind about the whole not sleeping with me yet bullshit. He's all weird because we're not committed, doesn't want to get any girls pregnant or whatever."

My brows shoot up, straight into my hairline. "What the hell does *that* mean?"

"It means he doesn't want to risk sleeping with any gold diggers who might trap him. You'd be surprised by all the baby mama drama surrounding athletes."

I stare, shocked. No, I did not know that happened. "He told you that?"

"Yeah, when he was drunk once at a party." She stops chewing, shaking a limp carrot stick in my direction. "Why are you looking at me like that?"

"Have you ever dated a guy because you genuinely

liked him, or do you just date them for their status?"

Her hesitation is a brief flicker. "Both?"

At least she's being honest.

I roll my eyes. They're a touch darker than hers, the left one with a fleck of amber in the corner. Our eyes are one of the few things that set us apart—a fact that she hates—and I also have a dimple in the corner of my lip.

"Name *one* guy you *really* liked."

She bites down on her bottom lip. It's pouty and pink. "This isn't a fair question, and why is it your business if I've never really liked anyone I've dated?"

"You're making it my business—hello, you want me to switch places with you and go on a date with some stranger." Who, quite frankly, I'm beginning to feel bad for. "If you liked him so much, you wouldn't be—"

"Dating someone else at the same time," we both say at the same time.

There is a hamburger on a plate in front of me getting cold, so I take a bite, chewing thoughtfully. "I didn't even know you were dating anyone, let alone *two* someones. In fact, I've never been introduced to any of your boyfriends since we've been in Iowa."

"It never gets to the point where we're serious," she counters. "And before you say anything, it's not my fault I get bored easily."

"Um, yeah, it kind of is." I'm talking with my mouth full. "Stop *using* guys and find one you *like*. Get to know one of them and maybe you won't get bored. Stop going out with athletes. Try dating someone with substance."

"Ew. That sounds like such a mind-numbing idea."

"Try it once, for me." I bat my lashes. "Pretty please."

"No. It's easy to sit here and judge me, isn't it?"

"What's that supposed to mean?"

"You've never dated a jock so you have no idea what you're missing. Oh my gawd, the orgasms—they are so worth the headache."

True, I have never dated a jock, but the orgasms I've had with other guys have been just fine, *thank you very much*, even if a bit ordinary.

"So will you do it?"

"What? No!" *Maybe.*

"Ugh, why are you like this?" my twin sister huffs, throwing her napkin on the table in a mini tantrum. "Help me! Please. You're the sweet one—maybe if you go out with him, he'll change his mind about me."

"Is that what this is about? Do you even have two dates on the same night?"

"Yes! I swear I have two dates next Friday night."

"Then how about you do the right thing and cancel one of them?"

Lucy glares across the table. "You're the worst freaking twin."

I laugh into my burger, taking a huge chunk off.

"We used to have so much fun, didn't we?" she tries again while my mouth is too occupied to argue.

I quickly chew and swallow. "Yes, it was fun—when we were *twelve*."

"Whatever, spoilsport."

I laugh. "Eat your lunch, I have class in ten minutes."

"For old time's sake? Please? Dash is harmless—really smart and levelheaded. You'll love him." Her smile curves innocently.

For the first time tonight, I pause, considering it. Set down my food, fiddle with a napkin, not meeting her eyes. "I'm listening."

"He's taking me to a battle of the bands, which you know is something I *hate*, but you *love* that kind of thing. My other date, Hudson, is taking me clubbing, which you know I love. I'm wearing that new silver dress I bought for New Year's Eve."

Hudson—what a dumb name.

"What if you end up having a date with Hudson for New Year's and he's already seen you in the silver dress?"

I smirk at the sight of her crestfallen expression.

"Shit. I hadn't thought of that."

"Yeah, well..." I shrug through her scowl. "That's what you have me for."

"Look, I'll make it easy: I'll drop off the outfit I'd planned to wear, and you won't have to worry about any details. Just get dressed and he'll show up."

"Where?" I'll admit to being a teensy weensy bit curious about where this date she doesn't want to go on is happening.

"The bar district, to listen to some local band."

"What kind of band?"

"I don't know Amelia! Some garage band or whatever. I was only half listening."

"Hmm." That sounds kind of fun. "What time?"

"Eight on Friday."

"And you don't think he'd notice that I'm not you?"

"No way, not a chance. He's a guy." Lucy leans in again. "Does this mean you'll do it?"

"I don't want to, but…"

She gets up from the table, comes around to my side, and puts me in a struggle cuddle from behind. "Yes! You are the best! I owe you big time.""I know you do."

She pokes a finger in my direction. "You can't tell Mom or Dad."

"Wouldn't dream of it." Pause. "I guess…have Dash pick me up on campus?"

"Can't you come to my house and have him pick you up there?"

"You're seriously going to push your luck? Have him pick me up on campus. I'll be in front of the field house."

"Amelia, he's going to think that's so weird."

"Ugh! Fine, fine. I'll be at your house at quarter to eight." I poke a finger back at her. "You better hope he's not early."

CHAPTER TWO

AMELIA

He's early.

Fifteen minutes early, to be exact, strolling up the sidewalk to my sister's house at the same exact time I am. My house is only a few short blocks away, so I hoofed it over, heels clicking on the cement below my feet.

As if this evening wasn't already extremely awkward for me, I'm approaching Lucy's at a snail's pace when I see a guy I assume is Dash already on her doorstep, poised to knock.

I stop short, halting on the pavement to watch him, the dark shrouding me as I hover under a tall maple tree like a total creep, considering my options while teetering on these heels Lucy brought over.

Stealing a few moments to observe, I have a mere second or two before he rings the doorbell or pounds on the door.

He's tall, with wide-set athlete's shoulders. I can see the planes of his muscles flexing beneath his t-shirt, highlighted by the dim porch lights on either side of Lucy's front door. Jet-black hair gleams when he shifts on his heels, raising his fist, knuckles ready to rap against the storm door.

"Dash?" I softly call out, testing the nickname on my lips, not wanting him to knock but not quite sure if this is Dash, or Hudson, or whoever my sister's date is for tonight.

I walk closer, clutching my purse, moving forward into the light.

"Lucy?"

"Yeah, it's me. I'm over here." I walk closer still, pasting on a smile, a knot forming in my stomach.

"Hey." He backtracks down the steps of the porch, jogging toward me. "What are you doing out here?"

He's close enough that I can see him better, nothing but strength and swagger. One look at his face and I begin stumbling over my words.

"Um, I was, uh…I had to…oh! I know!" *Jesus, Amelia, you've seen a cute guy before.* "I forgot I'd left my wallet at a friend's house? And I ran to get it. Didn't want to forget my ID, nope I did not!" I push out a laugh so fake I want to gag.

He cocks his head to the side, studying me, all high cheekbones and thick slashes of eyebrows. Beautiful dark skin, brawny…*God he's cute.* My sister wasn't kidding when she said he was good-looking.

What she didn't mention was that Dash Amado is Latino.

Muy caliente—very freaking hot.

"You need to run inside or anything?"

"Nah, I'm good. We can get going." So I can get this night over with, come home, get into my pajamas—preferably by ten o'clock at the latest—and forget this whole evening took place.

He clicks a remote hidden in his back pocket, unlocking the doors of his black car. Pulls the passenger side open, waits until I'm buckled in before closing the door with a dull thud. Jogs around the front to the driver's side.

I do a quick visual scan of the car's interior. It's clean, no garbage in the back seat, and smells like masculine aftershave and gym equipment. I peel my eyes off the bat bag in the back seat as Dash folds his big body inside.

"Sorry I'm a little early, but the band starts at eight fifteen and I wanted to get a spot in the front. Ready?"

Ready as I'll ever be, considering I haven't done the old switcheroo since I was a teenager.

"Yay! So ready," I reply in my best impression of Lucy.

He starts the engine, throwing on his blinker to enter traffic, overly cautious given there's virtually no traffic on this street. It is completely deserted.

"Thanks for going along with this." He glances over, large hands gripping the wheel. "When you asked me out, this was the best I could do on such short notice."

"Excuse me?"

Wait, did he just say *'when you asked me out'*?

I clear my throat and, as casually as I can, ask, "I asked you out?"

He glances sidelong across his shoulder, dark eyebrows raised. "You must have been drunker than I thought if you don't even remember asking me on a date." He chuckles. It's one of those low, sexy laughs you see played out in the movies, the ones that send a shiver down your spine while watching the romance unfold.

I want to shake that inconvenient shiver out through my shoulders, give my face a small slap.

"Must have been. You know me—fun, fun, fun! Always drunk on the weekends." *Shut up Amelia! Do you want him to think your sister is a lush?*

He shoots me another glance, this one slightly less enthusiastic, slightly more unamused. "Right."

I shift in my seat, the belt across my chest and lap constrictive, Lucy's tight denim jeans squishing my gut. I give them a tug at the waistband, looping my finger inside the fabric, pulling in an attempt to loosen the already stretchy material.

My shirt—one of her favorites—is off the shoulder, blue with thin white pinstripes and feminine bell sleeves. My collarbone has been dusted with gold, lips a beckoning dark burgundy (her words, not mine).

On my feet? Four-inch cork wedges.

I look sexy enough, I guess.

I'm terribly uncomfortable.

"You have to wear this shirt Amelia," my sister insisted, shoving the hanger into my hands. "Unless we want him noticing how much bigger my boobs have miraculously gotten in the course of four days." She dug through her closet like a stylist on a mission. "Your boobs are bigger than mine—I don't want Dash to think I stuff my bra."

"Lucy, no one stuffs their bra anymore."

When we're together, it's like an eye-rolling competition that has no victor.

"You know what I mean. Just put this on and act happy, okay? Smile and make sure you touch him a lot, or he'll think I'm acting funny."

I reach across the center console and tap his forearm flirtatiously.

"I remember asking you out, it just took me a second," I say in self-defense, trying to repair any damage I might have done to my sister's reputation by word-vomiting all over Dash's car. "And I do other things besides drink on the weekends."

His black brows rise again. "Like what?"

"Like...spending a lot of time with my sister. She goes here, too," I inform him, laying the ground work for Lucy to eventually break the news that she doesn't just have a sister—she has a twin.

"No shit?"

"We're *real* close."

"That's cool." His eyes are trained on the road, and he sounds bored. "What do the two of you do when you hang out?"

"Um..." We do *her* homework, talk. "Call our parents—we're from Illinois—and when the weather is nice, we ride bikes or go down by the lake."

"I can picture that." He smiles, turning left at a stop sign, heading to the tiny downtown district where all the bars are.

"What's the name of the band again?" I squeak out, sounding so unpolished and un-Lucy-like, it's positively *absurd.*

"Scotty's Tone Deaf."

"Oh. That...has a nice ring to it."

Dash laughs, pitching his head back, filling the interior of the car with his delicious baritone voice. "That's one way of putting it. We're basically going to listen to a garage band. There's a kid named Scotty who lives at the end of Jock Row with his parents," he offers by way of explanation as he pulls into the parking lot of The Warehouse, the city's only concert venue. "He's in high school and has a rock band, has this idol worship of the guys in the house."

"Including you?"

He bows his head, embarrassed. "*Sí.*" *Yes.*

"That's sweet." Pause. "Did you already tell me this?"

Jesus, I sound like a complete idiot; if Lucy finds out, she's going to kill me. Seriously, I need to stop talking before I make the whole thing worse.

I run down the facts Lucy gave me about Dash:

Twenty-two.

Six foot one.

Catcher on the baseball team.

Reserved.

Polite.

Lives on Jock Row in the baseball house.

That's it, the entire catalog of seven things I know about him, and most likely the only seven things my *sister* will *ever* know.

"You sure you're okay with listening to Scotty's band? I figured you'd be cool with it." He shoots me a perfect smile, his white teeth set off by his beautiful olive skin. "I wouldn't call this a concert, I'd call it a set. They're letting Scotty's band play a few songs before the battle begins, nothing major. He's the opening act before an opening act."

"I *love* that."

"Scott's in high school," he goes on. "I have no idea how he conned the manager of this place into letting him play, but I'm the only one from the house who promised to come listen."

"That is so nice of you. I'm looking forward to it."

I realize that I actually am. Dash has been a real gentleman so far, and I'm gradually beginning to ease up and enjoy his company.

He pulls into a parking space, puts the car in park, cuts the engine.

"I'd feel like a dick not showing up—the kid is only seventeen—but just so you know, there's a chance his band is going to seriously suck."

I grin at him, unable to stop myself. "*Or* he might surprise us?"

He's not convinced, yanking the keys from the ignition. "Maybe, but I doubt it."Still.

He brought me to watch his kid neighbor's band play—how sweet is that? My heart dips, and not because of the guilt I feel about deceiving this guy. Quite the opposite.

Dash Amado is not only amazingly hot.

He's amazing.

CHAPTER THREE

DANTE

I put my hand on the small of Lucy's back, guiding her through the front entry of The Warehouse after standing in line and buying two tickets. I lead her toward the stage; there's plenty of room near the front.

Or there are a few tables near the back.

I point to one as we pass it. "Should we go up front, or do you want a table?"

"We should definitely stand up front so he can see you." Lucy gives me a nudge with her elbow. "You want him to know you're here, don't you?"

I nod.

Steering her forward, my hand still lingering on the small of her spine, my restless fingers find that sweet spot on the curving slope down to her ass. The fabric of her shirt is soft; I allow myself the luxury of letting it run liquid along my palm before pulling my entire arm away.

She glances at me over her shoulder, long hair swinging.

It's definitely darker than the last time I saw her, and thicker?

When she smiles at me, I notice a small divot at the

corner of her mouth I hadn't noticed before, a tiny indentation near her full bottom lip.

I want to put the tip of my finger there and press it.

She catches me gaping at the dimple and touches it—covering it—offering me a wary, shy smile. Lucy, shy? No, that can't be right; this chick is a man-eater. She's the one who asked me out. She's the one who's always hanging all over me and my teammates at house parties, not the other way around.

She's aggressive.

Way more aggressive than I'm attracted to.

I don't know if I'm hallucinating, but the Lucy Ryan that showed up tonight? She's been acting uncharacteristically reserved since I found her loitering outside her house.

Once more, my eyes roam to the tiny indent near her mouth, lingering there.

Nope. That definitely *wasn't* there before.

Was it?

It's adorable—I'd definitely remember.

Wouldn't I?

Jesus Christ, estoy perdiendo la cabeza. I'm losing my damn mind.

We weave our way to position ourselves near the stage, early enough to score a great spot—dead center, right in the middle. Far enough up that Scotty will see me, far enough back that we can leave when the other bands play.

Unfortunately, we have to stand around for fifteen fucking more minutes waiting for this battle to begin, and Lucy doesn't strike me as the type who can engage in conversation stimulating enough to keep me interested for long, let alone a whole quarter of an hour.

I can suffer through small talk until the band starts.

It's our third date.

And our last.

After tonight, I doubt I'll ever take her out again. Girls like Lucy lack the refinement I want in a girlfriend—she's good for a quick fuck, maybe a few casual dates, but she won't *conocer a mi familia—meet my family.*

Mi madre would be fucking pissed if I brought a girl like her home.

Estaría muerto. I'd be dead.

Still…there's something about her tonight that has me second-guessing my first impressions, something I can't put my finger on.

Tonight she seems aloof. Conservative.

Pretty and polite.

Classy.

It's weird.

A *good* weird.

My lips curl into a smile as I look down at the crown of her head, the light hitting her hair, emphasizing the rich, chocolate brown color. Was it this color over the weekend? She must have gotten it dyed or whatever.

"Want anything to drink from the bar?" I lean into her, dipping my shoulders to get close, though she's tall enough with those high heels on.

"Hmm." She hesitates, worrying her lower lip. "Do I?"

I chuckle so low she couldn't possibly hear me over the noise. "I don't know, do you?"

"Are *you* drinking?"

What kind of a question is that? It's a weekend—of course I was planning on drinking. Unless…does she not *want* me to drink?

"I was gonna do a beer."

A firm nod. "Okay, that's what I'll have."

"Beer?" I feel my mouth twitch. "What kind?"

"Whatever kind you're having?"

"Are you sure?" She had white wine the last time we went out—four glasses of it, to be exact—and got shit-faced drunk. "I'm sure they have wine if you want it."

Her mouth moves, forming the words, "Shit, that's right. I drink wine, don't I?" The venue is loud and echoes, but her words are clear, perfectly formed on her lips. Lucy pauses indecisively. "I guess I'll have wine if they have it."

She looks less than thrilled, pouty even.

"Tell me what you want, and I'll grab it."

"Let's do wine." A curt nod. "I'm a wine drinker that happens to also love beer, but tonight I'll do wine, please."

My face, of its own free will, twists into a *would you make up your damn mind* expression, and I fight off an impatient groan and an irritable sigh. "You want to hold our spots while I head to the bar or come with me?"

"No, no, you go! I mean, sure—yes, I'll hold our spots," she enthuses, practically shooing me toward the bar, but not physically touching me. "Yup, you go. I'll wait here, right here in this spot. I won't go anywhere."

She flashes me a smile that's just a little too cheerful; if I didn't know any better, I'd think she was trying to get rid of me.

"All right," I say slowly. "Give me a minute. Be right back."

It takes me a solid five minutes to ease my way through the congested crowd to the bar, another five to hit the front of the line, and several more to get service.

One bottle of beer for me and one plastic cup of cheap white for her and I'm back at her side. When I sidle up, my date is furiously texting someone, head snapping up when she catches sight of me out of her periph. Shoves the phone in the back pocket of her jeans.

"Hey! I missed you!"

Plucking the cup of wine out of my hand, Lucy peers into it, squinting with one eye squeezed shut.

"Thanks." When she sips it, her lips pucker. "Bottoms up!"

I don't know why the hell she'd order it if she so obviously hates it, but I gave up trying to figure women out years ago.

"Good stuff?" I want to fucking laugh.

"Really good. Thank you." Lucy takes another labored sip, demonstrating just how tasty she finds it. "Mmm."

"If you don't want it, don't drink it."

"No! It's good. See?" Another gulp, another set of sour lips she's terrible at hiding.

"Lucy, why the hell would you order wine if you don't like it?" I pause, hold out my cup. "Do you want to chase it with some beer?"

She hesitates, glances behind us at the bar, which is now completely swarming with people. If I go back for another beer, it'll take another half hour and I'll miss Scotty's entire gig.

"Don't worry about it. This is fine."

I take a chug of my bottle of amber, offer it to her. "Want a drink of mine?"

Her hand goes up, waving in protest. "No, no, that's okay—don't worry about it."

"I'm not *worried* about it, but if you want a beer, I can share. It's not like we haven't swapped spit before."

The lighting in here is shit, but I swear to God, Lucy is blushing. Has to be by the way her head dips, unable to meet my eyes.

On stage, Scotty's band begins to saunter out, taking their places, running a sound check. The drummer inspects his kit; guitarists tune their strings. Lead singer taps the mic, raising and lowering it, tightening the screw to hold it at his preferred height.

As he's doing that, my neighbor kid looks up, catches sight of me, throws a peace sign at the same time he swings his black bass guitar strap around his neck like he's done it hundreds of times.

He probably has.

Well practiced, moving with ease, Scotty doesn't look nervous at all. In fact, the teenage shit gives me a cocky wink when they begin a warm-up, exercising their fretting hands.

Wearing the well-worn t-shirt of another popular band and torn jeans, Scott bends his knees, strumming, hair gelled into tiny spikes.

Their first cords are upbeat.

First words, in tune.

Fluid.

Soon, I find my head bobbing to the beat. Lucy and I pass the beer back and forth between us, tipping it back. It goes down cold and smooth, but it's not enough for two.

I grasp for it again, prepared to take another swig.

"Wait! Does this not taste so damn good? God I love it when they're cold."

Her eyes close when she swallows.

Her hips sway when the music begins.

It's pretty fucking great.

***

AMELIA

I'm not expecting the next song to be slow, just like I'm not expecting my body to sway, hips gently rocking to the music.

I haven't had much to drink, but it's enough to loosen me up and forget myself, if only for a few moments. Enough for me to enjoy the company and the big, warm palms that slide around my waist.

It's a full house tonight, stuffy.

"*¿Está bien?*" *Is this okay?* "Sorry I keep bumping into you, but the dickhead behind us keeps knocking into me." His smooth voice speaks into my ear, the rich sound of his Spanish hitting all the nerves in my spine. "*Te sientes diferente—una diferencia buena.*"

You feel different, he says, rolling his tongue. A good different.

Since I'm pretending to be my twin sister—who doesn't know a lick of Spanish—I don't acknowledge the words, giving a feeble little nod without betraying myself.

In reality? My entire body is in complete and utter chaos.

I can understand him—*perfectly.*

I don't want Dash speaking Spanish in my ear, whispering words meant for someone else. I don't want Dash touching me—not because he repulses me.

But because he doesn't.

He's the antithesis of everything I thought he'd be. For the sake of my sanity, and to get me through this farce of a fake date, I desperately hoped the guy walking through my sister's door would be a jerk.

A jockhole.

I prayed he'd be a stereotype, a caricature of what I perceive the average student athlete on our college campus to be. My sister is the jersey chaser, not me.

Pompous.

Boorish.

Egotistical asshole.

Dante Amado is none of those things.

He's easygoing. Kind. Personable.

Every gentlemanly gesture out of Dash Amado has been sincere. His nice-guy routine is not an act; it's who he is.

His mama raised him right.

And I'm so confused by it.

I wasn't prepared for him to be like this.

Dammit! I'm not supposed to be attracted to my sister's boyfriend— the guy my sister is *dating*—no matter how serious it isn't, no matter how good-looking he is.

Honestly? I kind of hate myself right now.

A knot of guilt twists inside my stomach at the same time Dash's hands ease around my waist, sliding over my rib cage, giving me a little squeeze. If I had to speak, there's no way I'd be able to form a cohesive sentence.

The knot gets heavier, tighter, weighing me down. I'm the world's worst twin.

The world's worst *sister*.

"Having fun?" His baritone vocals hit my cerebellum, shockwaves finding their way down to all my best girly parts. "I really thought they were going to sound like complete shit—thank God they don't."

My throat is tight, and I have to clear it before I can speak. "I'm really impressed—I can't believe they're in high school."

As many times as I've told myself I would try to fill Lucy's high-heeled shoes on this date, I'm failing—*so miserably*. I want so desperately to be myself. I want my damn body to stop responding to Dash Amado. I want my damn heart to stop beating so wildly it feels like it's about to burst out of my chest.

If only my cheeks weren't so flushed, my palms so sweaty.

I'm a complete mess.

Dash's giant catcher's paws grip my body, loosely resting on my hips, thumbs hooking inside the front pockets of Lucy's jeans.

He lowers his head, gently resting his chin on my

shoulder, lips intermittently brushing against the exposed skin of my jawline as he stares straight ahead, watching Scotty.

I let my lids flutter closed, allowing my lashes to rest on my cheekbones for the briefest of seconds, giving myself this one moment.

This is how it would feel if we were a couple.

It feels too good.

He feels good.

So good. "Tan bueno," I say, forgetting myself, muttering out loud. *"Tan bueno."*

Dash goes still.

"¿Que es tan bueno?" His mouth is right there, lips grazing my neck. *What's so good?* he wants to know.

Jesus, it's driving me absolutely freaking crazy—the Spanish, his cologne and his breath and the heat from his body. Even the hair on his arms is giving me goose bumps, the baby fine strands tickling the skin of my forearms as his thumbs dig gently into my hips.

"Huh?" I ask in a daze.

"You said *so good.*"

"Mmm, nope. Don't think so."

"Yes you did." His lips skim the shell of my ear, speaking in a foreign language I spent years mastering. "I heard you, and you said it in Spanish."

"I did?"

"¿Hablas español, Lucy?" Do you speak Spanish?

What the hell am I supposed to say to that? My sister doesn't speak a word of it. "Um...?"

"¿Qué más no me estás diciendo?" What else aren't you telling me? *"Be honest."*

"Nothing." Shit, I just answered him again.

He pulls back, turns me to face him, lightly setting those massive palms on my bare shoulders, fingers spreading over my skin, guaranteed to leave scorch marks in their wake.

His fingers brush the hair off my collarbone.

"¿Puedes entenderme?" You can understand me?

Crappers.

"Sí." I cast my eyes away, chastised.

His are too intense.

Something changes in his expression then; he studies me under the lights of the stage, the red, blue, and green flickering strobes casting a glow across his skin.

Across mine.

Dash can't quite figure me out, and I don't blame him; I'm acting like I have multiple personalities. How could I let that Spanish slip out? Lucy is guaranteed to be pissed about that once she finds out.

Lucy, who could barely do her own English papers in high school.

I'm not my sister.

Not even close.

And call me crazy, but for a fleeting moment while Dash stands watching me—learning my tells—his brows lower and rise, concentrating on my face, reading every line imprinted there, eyes traveling over my chest, hair, and face.

The corner of my mouth.

In an instant, he knows.

He just doesn't *know* that he knows.

And he's confused.

"Come on." He bends now, talking loud. "We need to talk. Let's go grab another beer."

"Where?" I shout back.

Those mammoth shoulders shrug. "What about the bar? At the back of the room? We'll be able to hear each other better."

"Okay. Sure." I think I'd follow him anywhere.

Dash takes my hand without hesitating, without asking for permission, weaving us through the crowd, and I follow, fingers wrapped around his tightly.

My lifeline.

He gives them a squeeze, lacing them together, glancing back at me over his broad shoulders. It's then that I realize: I'm not paying attention to where I'm walking; I'm just watching *him*.

The muscles in his strong back contract as he works his way through the crowd. His thick neck corded, sexy. I've always liked that part of a guy's body, always found it attractive.

Masculine.

My hungry eyes rake down his backside, down his tapered waist, over his firm ass, and I allow myself the luxury of *every* part of him, pretending the large hands and imposing form tugging me along belong to me.

Pretending he's mine for the taking.

We reach the bar, where the crowd has thinned out considerably since the music started, the sound of Scotty's band blasting through the subwoofers and speakers drowning out any laughter and loud chatter.

Dash orders us beer, ice water.

Faces me while we wait, one arm resting on the bar top.

I wonder how long it's going to take for him to bring up the fact that I speak Spanish.

For now, he seems content to stand here surrounded by the concertgoers, the loud music, and my quiet company. If he thinks it's strange that I, as Lucy, finally have nothing to say, he would be right. My sister is always chattering away, and she'd be talking non-stop right now, too.

The only things *I* can think of to ask Dash are personal; I want to know more about him, want to know things that are none of my business.

Does he have brothers or sisters?

Where is he from?

What's his major? What does he want to be if he doesn't play baseball after he graduates?

Are these things he and my sister have already talked about?

We stand at the bar, regarding each other, his cool black gaze caressing my exposed shoulders. I respond to it by coolly lifting the beer bottle to my lips and taking another drink of liquid courage, hoping to avoid his disconcerting scrutiny.

I don't know what it is, but Dash is someone I want to get to know more, someone I'd want to know if the circumstances were different.

I sigh.

The fact is that tonight, I am not supposed to be myself.

And I'm doing a really crappy job being my sister.

"So, you wanna tell me what's going on with you?"

"What do you want to know?"

CHAPTER FOUR

DANTE

L ucy speaks Spanish.

And not just the *I was required to take two years of it in high school* version. She actually knows how to fucking speak it, fluently.

I don't know what to do with this strange new information. It's certainly a game changer; I've never dated anyone who could have a conversation with me in any language other than English, and it's really fucking sexy.

We're sidled up to the bar, my arm draped on the lacquered wooden top, elbow propping me up as I study her.

Study her in a new light, riveted.

This Lucy isn't just a pretty face.

This Lucy isn't just a grasping jock chaser.

This Lucy has *layers*.

This version fascinates me more than the two versions that came before her.

Her striped baby blue shirt is understated but sexy, hair still falling in loose waves despite the growing humidity from all the warm bodies inside this packed concert hall.

Wavering unsteadily on high heels, she leans against

the counter, mimicking my stance, mimicking the way I let my gaze trail over her, returning the favor.

She peruses me up and down, expression unreadable.

It's so fucking unsettling.

Lo amo. I love it.

"So, you wanna tell me what's going on with you?"

"What do you want to know?"

"I think you know what I'm talking about. I've never met a single person on this campus who speaks Spanish as well as you seem to, besides other Latinos."

"I spent a semester in Mexico teaching English at an immersion school."

That makes no fucking sense. Lucy is a fashion major—why would she be teaching classes in Mexico?

"Why do you keep staring at me like that?"

The beer bottle hits my bottom lip and I tip it. Chug. "I'm trying to figure you out."

"I know," she returns unhappily. "Please don't."

"Are you intentionally trying to be evasive?"

"I'm not playing games with you, I promise, but it's complicated."

The bartender finally gets to us, setting two new bottles on the counter. Lucy reaches for one, taking a dainty sip, delicate fingers wrapped around the long neck of the bottle. Nails painted baby blue, the second to last one a glittery silver.

"You know Luce, I'm really fucking busy with school and baseball, so I don't date a lot, and this right here is why: I can't stand drama."

"Neither can I," she volleys back. "Maybe I'm just not good at this, did you ever think of that?"

"Not good at what?"

"Relationships. I've never dated a single guy for more than two weeks."

"Well that's good to know."

Her eyes roll toward the ceiling dramatically. "This is only your third date—I can't even believe we're discussing this."

This is only *your* third date? That's an odd way to put it.

"Besides," she continues, "aren't you ballplayers all just looking for a little fun between seasons?"

"I'm not a stereotype, but thanks."

Her expression falls. "I didn't mean it like that. I'm just...I'm not comfortable having this conversation with you right now."

"Why?"

"Because I...it's..." She's reluctant to finish her sentence. "It's personal."

"You know, Lucy, relationships don't usually work when one person is hiding something." Jesus, why am I trying so damn hard with this girl? I couldn't stand her the last time we went out, and I'm only here with her tonight so I didn't have to come alone.

"*Hiding* something?" Her eyes are wide. "What would make you say that?"

"You're either really good at faking who you are, or you have no fucking clue what you want." I can't describe the look on her face right now, couldn't if I tried, not for a million fucking bucks. It's a cross between crestfallen and oddly captivated...stricken but expectant?

Like she wants to cry and laugh all at the same time.

So bizarre. "Why are you staring at me like that?"

Lucy swallows a lump in her throat, eyes shining. "I literally just asked you that same thing, so how am I staring at *you*?"

"Like you're dying to say something."

Her chin tips up, that little dimple by her bottom lip drawing attention to itself, imprinted in her skin.

My eyes fixate on it, narrowing. "I'm not fucking stupid. Something weird is going on with you, and I want to know what it is."

"Nothing *weird* is going on." Her nostrils flare, eyes get bright. "I have *no* idea what you're talking about."

"So it's going to be like that, huh?"

Her arms cross. "What do you think is weird?"

"To avoid the risk of feeling like a fucking dumbass, I'd rather not bring it up, okay?"

She's in my space now, fingers splayed on my forearm. "*Tell* me."

"Your hair is different," I blurt out.

"How?"

Jesus Christ, this is going to sound so stupid. "It's longer...and darker." I go for broke. "And I swear you didn't have this the last time I saw you."

I extend my arm, placing my finger on that perfect spot by her mouth. Her dark lips part.

Lucy's breath catches. Something in her eyes...

"What else?" she whispers.

"Your—" My eyes drop to her breasts then rise again. I'm such a fucking hornball. "Never mind."

Behind us, Scotty's band interrupts, striking another chord, his adolescent voice croaking into the microphone. "This is going to be it for us tonight, Bettys and gents. One last lullaby before the big show. Enjoy, and have a great fucking night."

The slow rifts of guitars still the crowd.

Still Lucy.

Her lips are curved smugly. "Were you going to say my boobs look bigger?"

There's no getting out of this one; she totally caught me checking out her tits, which I can barely see beneath her blousy top. "Maybe."

"What if you were right?" The words fall out of her mouth before her lips clamp shut. "Please forget I said that."

Yeah…not happening.

Lucy clears her throat. "So should we—"

"Dance? Sure." Why the hell not? Everyone else is.

Neither of us smile, but she lets me take her beer bottle and set it on the bar, lead her to the edge of the ballroom floor where the concert crowd is gathered, couples dancing to little Scotty's kickass garage band.

My hands catch skin when they slide around Lucy's waist, accidentally skimming above the waistband of her jeans. I let my fingers stroke the skin of her ribcage before they behave, dragging back down to the swell of her denim-clad hips.

Tentatively, her hands run up the front of my black t-shirt; it's the second time she's touched me tonight, and her warm palms, with their pretty blue nails, are doing some seriously fucked up shit to my libido as they settle on my chest.

Her chin tips up so she can look in my eyes. "You realize you finished my sentence before, and I finished yours?"

"We did?"

"Yes. No one ever does that with me except my sister."

I have nothing to add to that.

"Scott is great." She breaks the silence, fingers toying with the cotton of my shirt. "Does he come around your house often?"

"Yeah, just about every week. He plays ball, and he's mildly obsessed with our pitcher, Rowdy Wade."

"Rowdy, Dash—do you all have nicknames?"

"We call some guys by their last names."

"And you get yours because you're fast?" Affirmative. "But you're a catcher...how does that work?"

Does she not know anything about baseball?

"Everyone on the team has a turn at bat, and when my bat connects with the ball, I run like hell."

The song Scotty's band plays is actually really fucking haunting. Beautiful.

Just like Lucy.

My arms move from her hips to her waist, pulling her in so we're flush, her palms sliding down from my pecs, smoothing themselves across my shoulders, brushing imaginary lint away. I want to kiss her and we both fucking know it; I've been dying to put my mouth on that dimple of hers.

I home in on it.

"Where did this suddenly come from?" I tease, bringing my hand up to float my thumb over the tiny indent, back and forth, unintentionally brushing the satiny flesh of her bottom lip. "I swear this wasn't here last time."

"I-I don't think we should do this," she protests against my finger, lids fluttering shut when my thumb caresses her cheek. "Maybe we should go back to the bar and finish our beer."

"Hey, it's all right." My brows rise. "We're just dancing."

My fingers trace her jaw, slipping to the back of her neck, raking through her soft hair. Her eyes meet mine, a thousand words I know she wants to say shining up at me, but it's nothing I'll hear out loud. This girl has secrets she doesn't want me finding out, and I want to know what they are.

I lower my head, intending to—

"I don't think you should kiss me."

I pull back, eyebrows drawn together, perplexed. "Why?"

"Because I want you to," the whisper slides out, a confession.

"That makes no sense."

"I know," she moans miserably.

"You want to kiss me, but you don't—got it." I'm tenderly stroking her skin with the palm of my hand, the calloused pads learning the contours of her face. "You don't care if I do this in the meantime, do you? Until you change your mind?"

"I'm not going to change my mind."

Lowering my face to the crook of her neck, I trail my nose up the pillar of sweet skin, letting my mouth tag along for the ride. My wet tongue meets her flesh and I want to gently suck, but don't. I nip instead. "Is this okay? No kissing on the lips," I whisper into her ear. "Just like in *Pretty Woman*."

"F-F…" she stutters. "Fine. Sure, whatever. Just not on the lips."

What a little weirdo.

My laughing mouth finds the pulse in the slim column of her neck, and I'm satisfied when she tilts her head to one side, hair falling like a waterfall over her shoulder, giving me all the access I want and need.

Grasping her hand, my fingers flutter lightly along the length of her arm before I raise it, kiss the inside of her wrist, the pale skin a stark contrast to my own.

Dragging my mouth along the smooth flesh of her forearm, up and down the inside of her elbow. Lucy holds perfectly still.

"*¿Todavía no quieres que te bese en los labios?*" *Still don't want me to kiss your lips?*

One jerky shake of her head.

"No?"

Another shake. *No.*

"Jesus, Luce, you're killing me here," I murmur against her mouth, our lips an inch apart, so close our breaths mingle. I wish our tongues were, too.

"It's killing me too. I'm sorry."

That's the second time she's apologized, so I kiss the tip of her nose, leaning in to whisper, "Don't be."

"God Dash, don't do that," she whispers back, stroking the back of my head, wrapping my black hair around her finger.

Chest heaving, her hands unhurriedly flutter up and down the bulk of my biceps, breasts pressed against my chest as she moves closer.

This non-kissing, sexual tension-filled bullshit is better than any fucking kiss I've ever had on the mouth, that's for damn sure. It's giving me a raging boner, body hard as a rock when she arches her back.

"Don't do what?" My murmured question makes her shiver. Goose bumps form across her skin.

"Don't be so…" Lucy deliberates, choosing her words.

"Irresistible?"

"Sure, we'll go with that."

We take the moment to stare at each other, and I swear to fucking God, it's like we're seeing each other for the first damn time. My hands embrace her jawline as her fingers clench my wrists.

"Lucy."

The air between is pulled taut, intensely so.

Buzzing.

Sizzling.

"Dash, please don't." I can't hear her words, but I can see them, and it's enough to stop myself from doing something really fucking dumb, like kissing her senseless, which is taking some superhero-level self-restraint on my part.

She moves first, burying her head in my chest as the music comes to an end, the crowd around us going wild, chanting and cheering for the band, for Scotty, the kid who practices in his parents' garage and tries to hang out with guys too old for him.

"We should go," comes her muffled mumble. "I need to go."

Need to go.

We pull apart, reluctantly. I could eat her up—and out—all fucking night long.

Instead, I release her.

"All right. Let's get you home."

CHAPTER FIVE

AMELIA

D*zzt. Dzzt.*
      Dzzt.

It's barely six thirty in the morning when my phone begins buzzing, vibrating against my bedside table, an entire hour before I have to be up to get to my study group.

I reach for it, finger blindly searching for the *end* button but accidentally hitting *accept*. Dammit all, what's my sister doing calling so freaking early?

The last time she woke me at this hour was two Christmases ago when she and our brother, Dexter, were up at the butt-crack of dawn—like children—so they could open their presents.

My siblings, bless their hearts, are early risers.

I, however, am not.

"Luce?" My voice is raspy, sounding eerily similar to someone gasping for a last breath. "Is everything okay?"

"No, everything is not okay. Are you still in bed?" It's an accusing tone, one I simply don't have the patience for at this hour of the damn day.

I blink into the sunlight just beginning to pour through my bedroom window, rising to sit, propped against my headboard. Worried, I squint toward the clock. "What's wrong? Why are you calling so ungodly early? Did something happen to Mom or Dad?"

"Oh jeez, don't be so dramatic." I hear the sound of the wind hitting the mouthpiece of her phone, an indication that she's outside, probably getting ready for a run or something equally horrifying.

Mollified that there's no emergency, I flop back onto my side, hunkering down. Grumble, "What do you want?"

"How did it go last night?"

"Fine?"

"And?"

"And nothing. It went fine."

"My dates don't ever go 'fine'. They're either fantastic or awful. So which was it?"

"I can't even function right now. How are you this chipper?"

"Why aren't you answering the question?" I swear I can hear her stop dead in her tracks. "Is there something you're not telling me?"

My body goes still. "Why would you ask me that?"

"Twintuition." She sniffs into the phone. "I *felt* it last night while I was with Hudson."

Hudson. I still cannot get over that name.

"Oh Lord."

"You had fun, didn't you? You never texted me last night, so I was worried." Through the line, she worries her bottom lip, a trait that always gave us away; Lucy would always chew her bottom lip while we were getting yelled at, like she's doing now. "He wasn't being a jerk, was he?"

Despite how groggy I am, my brows rise. "Is he normally a jerk?"

"No?"

"Why are you saying it like it's a question? Don't you know?"

"I've only been out with him twice, Amelia. I guess he can be kind of an asshole when he's with his friends?" I imagine her bending down to re-tie her shoes. "So was he one with you?"

"No." Not at all. He was perfect.

"Yeah, I know. I just wanted to see what you'd say." She sounds satisfied. "I *felt* it."

"Honest to God, would you please stop saying that?" She is so annoying sometimes, especially before seven AM. "You're making me mental."

She ignores me. "How long were you out?"

"I don't know, I think I got home around one?"

"Really, that late?" Her air of approval is palpable. "What else?"

"Well, I mean, after he dropped me off at your place, I had to walk home." I sound begrudged. "In the dark."

"Yeah, yeah. Did he try to kiss us?"

Jesus. "Kind of."

"Did we let him?"

"No, but it was a pretty hardcore dodge and weave." *And I wanted him too, so badly.* We're both dead silent, waiting for my answer. "There's something I should probably tell you." I take a deep breath and confess, "I accidentally spoke Spanish with him last night."

Ten bucks says Lucy is wrinkling her nose at me. "He speaks Spanish?"

"Are you kidding me right now? Yes he speaks Spanish—he's Latino. Do you pay attention to anyone but yourself?"

"Sue me for not knowing, jeez. Tell me what was said and how it pertains to me, and do it quickly—I haven't started my run yet and I'm freezing my ass off out here."

"I had a *conversation* with him in *Spanish*, Luce." And the whole thing was so freaking sexy. The Rs rolling off his tongue...the deep timbre of his accent...

"Wait a minute." My twin inhales a breath, catching on. "Did you forget the small fact that I don't speak any Spanish! God Amelia, why would you do that to me?" my sister shouts through the phone. I pull it away from my ear, tapping down on the volume button.

"It just slipped out! I'm sorry, I got caught up in the moment."

"Caught up in the moment? What the hell were you guys doing? I thought you went to a concert—no one talks at concerts!"

"We did go to a concert! But he was saying stuff and it was so sweet, it just felt natural to reply in Spanish, and then one thing led to another and we were having a conversation."

"I don't understand how it just slipped out," she intones sarcastically.

I roll my eyes. "I doubt I have to explain how *alluring* he is, Lucy. You've been out with him twice—do you blame me?" Crap, that was totally inappropriate. "Sorry, I didn't mean to say that."

"Uh...if you like this guy, just tell me, Amelia."

"What would make you think I like him?" I want to face-palm myself with an anvil.

"You just said he was *alluring*. Who uses words like that?"

"I do."

"Hmm."

"You woke me up—what do you want me to say?"

The thing about my sister—no matter how flighty or vain or selfish she can be—is that she always wants what's best for me. I know I'm not going back to sleep until we talk this out.

"The entire time I was out with Hudson last night, I kept getting these niggling vibes," she begins slowly, enunciating every word. "Like, the whole damn time. I could barely concentrate on my date."

I hate when she does this.

I hate when she's right.

It's creepy.

"Your twintuition is wrong."

I'm lying and we both know it.

"Do you know," she begins thoughtfully, "he's been texting me since late last night, then again this morning, and now I know why half of them were in Spanish. I couldn't freaking understand most of them, and I'm not about to Google translate a text conversation."

"Oh? He texted you? That's good." I'm dying inside, doing my best to sound nonchalant despite this frantically beating heart.

The line goes quiet.

"Luce? What did he say?"

"The usual."

She's going to make me work for it.

"Which is what? I have no idea what the usual is."

"Well, for *one* thing—and please don't ever repeat this—Dash has never texted me before. Normally I'm the one sending him texts, which is so annoying. I hate when guys are like that. I hate having to message them first. I'm only admitting that to you because you're my sister and I forced you to go out with him."

I hate myself for asking, but, "Like…what else was he saying?" *About me.*

A loud sigh from the other end of the line. "I don't remember, Amelia. *Stuff.* The point *is*, he must have thought I was acting like a complete freak, 'cause he asked if I was feeling better and said maybe it was a mistake taking me to a concert, said he regrets how it was impossible to talk, blah blah blah. So annoying, don't you think? Anyway," she continues without letting me answer, "thanks for doing such a crap job as my stand-in that he thought I was sick. You could have made out with him to be a little more convincing. He's so hot."

"I was doing you a favor!" My mouth gapes open. "You should've thought about that when you *begged* me to be *you* for the night so you could go out with some guy name Hudson. *Hudson*—seriously, what kind of a name is that?"

"He—"

I don't let her get two words in before interrupting. "What did you *think* was gonna happen last night Lucy? With a guy like that, who has feelings—yeah, real feelings. He might be crazy good-looking, but he was really great, so yeah, the

Spanish just came flying out because I hardly get to practice anymore, and you're just going to have to deal with it."

"What the heck am I supposed to do? He's going to say all this shit I'm not going to understand."

Not to sound callous, but, "You don't even like the guy!"

"How do you know?"

"If you liked Dash, you would have gone out with him and not *Hudson*." I can barely get the guy's name out.

There's a long stretch of silence on the other end of the line, and I wonder what's going through her mind right now as she formulates a reply. It's either that or she's stretching, prepping for her run.

"You're right. You are totally, one hundred percent right." I can hear the revelation taking over her speech and brace myself. "I should break it off. I like Hudson way better. He gave me two orgasms last night, Amelia—two, *with his mouth*."

My mouth falls open, at a loss for words. "Lucy, how can you do that? That's cheating!"

"Calm down, Miss Priss. It's not like I knew I liked Hudson better before I double-booked myself. I had to sample the goods first." She laughs cheerfully. "And thanks to you, I know how I feel! So no, it's not like cheating. I'll text Dash as soon as we hang up and dump him."

My mouth falls open. "You're going to break up with him over *text*?"

I can hear my sister studying her nails, bored with our conversation, maybe even picking at the split ends of her long hair as she stands out on the sidewalk. "Well it's not like I'm going to *see* him any time soon, and I don't feel like going on another date with him."

Why doesn't she like him? Why would she do this? This superficial young woman is not the sister I know. It's those damn sorority girls she's hanging out with.

She's being callous and insensitive, and I don't like it.

Stay out of it Amelia, my inner voice shouts. This is none of your business. Stay out of it before you say something you'll regret, like how Dash is a great guy who smells amazing, is sweet in an unassuming way, and is too handsome for his own good.

And yet I can't help but add, "He's a nice guy—don't you think he deserves to be told in person? Isn't that what you would want if someone was breaking up with you?"

There's a long pause, then the loud sigh my sister is famous for in our family. "Honestly? No, not really. If someone was breaking up with me, why would I want to see their *face*?"

"Because—"

Whatever I'm about to say gets cut off when Lucy interrupts me. "Look, I have to start my run if I'm going to finish on time and keep my day on track."

"Fine," I huff.

"But if this is so damn important to you, why don't *you* break up with him for me? That saves me the trouble of doing it."

"Going on a date with him was bad enough. I did a terrible job pretending to be you, and there is no way I'll be able to look him in the eye and dump him for you."

She pauses. "Hold on, someone just texted me."

"Lucy! We're in the middle of a conversation!"

The phone is silent as she pulls it away from her ear to check it. "That was Dash—again. I just texted him back and told him I'd meet him at Zin downtown tomorrow night at seven. You can break up with him then."

"Lucy!" I shout, beyond exasperated. "I'm not breaking up with him for you!"

"Suit yourself." Her voice is flippant. "I have no problem texting him."

My stomach drops, a lead weight of guilt burdening me. "Don't hang up! Okay, okay, I'll do it. I'll break up with him for you."

She smiles on the other end of the line; I can hear it from here. "Thank you sissy. You won't regret this."

But she's wrong.

I already do.

CHAPTER SIX

AMELIA

I can't decide: what does a person wear to break up with their sister's boyfriend? A sweatshirt and jeans? A flirty top? Something dressier, because technically this could be considered a business meeting?

Khakis?

I stand in front of my closet, mid-panic, discarding one unsuitable shirt after another onto my bed, when what I should have done was force Lucy to choose a breakup outfit for me, like how she dressed me for the concert, since theoretically, I'm posing as her again.

Floral blouse? Way too fun.

Hot pink sweater? No—I'd die from heat stroke before I died from mortification.

No, no, and no—three more shirts join the others then out of the corner of my eye, I spot a dressy black turtleneck and impulsively yank it off its hanger.

Hold it up, inspecting it.

Prim. Proper.

Black.

Serious.

The perfect shit to wear if I was attending a funeral.

I slide it over my frame. It's fitted, hugging all my curves, and yet, the perfect metaphor: my attendance at the death of my sister's relationship with Dash Amado.

Don't get me wrong, I might be on my way to give the guy his marching orders, but I don't want to look like a complete frump.

Still.

I need to look and feel businesslike, and this onyx turtleneck is textbook professional. I'll appear efficient, organized, and…

Now I sound like a lunatic.

With a sigh befitting my twin, I shimmy and stumble into a pair of dark wash jeans, feet sliding into black half boots, give my hair a quick tussle, swipe on some gloss, and—*oh my God, I'm primping*. I'm trying to look nice.

Which is so not the point!

"Stop it, Amelia, this is not a date," I chastise myself, glaring into the mirror, angry. Rest my hands on either side of my dresser, looking my reflection in the eye. "Why are you doing this? You *like* him. You cannot pull this off."

I rise to my full height, puffing out my chest. "Yes you can. You can do this. You've broken up with guys before. Hell, you've broken up with *Lucy's* boyfriends before."

Twice, in high school.

I felt braver back then than I do now.

What's done is done; Lucy is out with Hudson tonight, and I'm on my way to meet Dash. There's no turning back.

I can only move forward.

***

He's late.

At seven o'clock sharp, I watch, engrossed as a large figure emerges through the door of Zin. I'm waiting with baited breath, watching when he tosses his head to get the hair out of his eyes.

Everything about Dash Amado is dark: his black quilted jacket, his jet-black hair, his complexion.

He flashes a friendly grin to the bartenders when he walks past, toward me, his pearly whites a stark contrast against his skin. Dark. Smooth. Handsome.

Through the dim lighting in the wine bar, I watch him peel off his jacket, sauntering his way over, surveying the crowd. There aren't many people here tonight so it's not long before our gazes connect.

In a few strides he's at my side, sliding onto the barstool next to mine, kissing the top of my head. "Hey. Sorry I'm late. I had to see the trainer—he was showing me a new way to wrap my wrists."

I can't stop my eyes from glancing down. I raise my brows, curious.

"They're not wrapped right now, just for practice." He cuffs his wrist with one hand, rubbing it. "Have you been here long?"

"I walked in just a few minutes early, so no. It's no big deal, the bartenders were keeping me company." Totally something Lucy would say, only she'd add a flirtatious smile, maybe touch his sleeve.

"Speaking of which, I'm thirsty." His lean torso leans across the bar, long arm snatching a drink menu before flagging down one of the bartenders. His eyes flicker to the water glass in front of me. "Do you want anything else or are you sticking with water?"

"Water is good." I'm here to do a job and need a clear mind. Drinking would be a horrible idea, though I may need a drink at the end of the night, maybe a shot or two, or three.

Dash nods down at my beverage, speaking to the guy behind the bar as he strolls over, drying a glass. "I'll have what she's having, and an iced tea if you have it? Thanks."

Whatever words I'm about to say get caught in my throat when he spins in his seat to face me, chugging down almost all of his glass of ice water, Adam's apple bobbing. Shaved neck, dark sideburns.

Dear Lord he's good-looking.

His eyes slide up and down the front of my shirt, landing briefly on my breasts. Lips quirk. "Nice turtleneck."

I can't decide if he's being sarcastic.

"I like turtlenecks. They're warm," I croak out, body blazing like an inferno, wanting to hook my index finger in the collar of my shirt and give it a tug. Yank it off, up over my head. Get it off my body, hating it.

His black brows go up. "I said I liked it. I wasn't being a dick."

"Oh. Well…thanks, I guess."

I've never been this nervous in my entire life, not even when I took my sister's college entrance exam.

He regards me over the top of his iced tea, the lemon wedge moving up and down like a jellyfish in the ocean.

"You look good though. *Muy bueno.* I think I like this shirt better than the one you wore on Friday night."

"Really?" I run a hand over my stick-straight hair, which I let air-dry after my shower. I'm hardly wearing any makeup, just some lip gloss—basically, my attempt at looking serious.

"You can't even see my neck." You can't see *anything*. This shirt is a protective layer between us; I don't want to feel sexy or attractive or pretty when I'm here to complete a task.

And yet...the goof likes it.

"Sí."

I like the way he's staring, taking my measure. I love the way he talks, the sound of his voice, even if he's not really talking to *me*.

The thought is sobering, and I gaze down at the shiny bar top despondently, picking at the corner of the white cocktail napkin under my glass of water. *Zin, a wine bar in downtown Iowa City – drink old wine, date young men.*

I study the slogan, running my fingers over the burgundy embossed writing, the texture of the paper feeling coarse under my fingertips.

Over and over it, around the cursive lettering.

He's still watching me when I look up.

"Should we have them seat us somewhere? I'm starving."

Hesitantly I nod, hopping down off the barstool, aware of just how big he is, how imposing.

Chest like a wall of steel, I bump into it inadvertently when I stand, apprehensively gathering my purse and coat from the stool, nerves making my palms sweaty.

I'm about to break up with my sister's boyfriend.

I already feel terrible for what I'm about to do—not because I think they'd make such a great couple, but because I like spending time with him, and once I tell him it's over between him and Lucy…

I'll probably never see him again.

Nonetheless, I trail along after him toward the hostess stand, idly waiting as he requests a table.

For two.

In the back corner.

When we're seated, Dash leans in, setting his hands on the table, moving aside his fork and knife and the rest of the utensils. "Can I be brutally honest with you?"

Please don't. "Sure."

"The first few times we went out, I wasn't feeling it at all."

"What do you mean?"

"You know I only went out with you because you're the one who asked, right? I never would have asked you out."

This surprises me, and I rear back in my seat, slightly affronted—and embarrassed—on my sister's behalf.

What do I even say to that?

"Before you get offended, let me finish what I was going to say."

Because I have nothing to say, I nod. "Okay."

"I haven't dated much. Since you're familiar with the Latino culture, you've probably guessed I come from a really traditional family. *Mis padres* raised me to be in a monogamous relationship, not sleep around, *¿sabes lo que* *digo?" Know what I mean?* he asks, tan, masculine hands picking apart a napkin, the tiny white pieces like snow on the black tabletop. "Anyway, I figured we'd go out a few times and that would be it."

"But?" I prod, shifting uncomfortably in my seat.

"Listen, you don't exactly scream 'relationship type'." His use of air quotes makes me blush, though I shouldn't take it personally since he's not actually speaking about me. "But I had a really great fucking time with you on Friday, Lucy. I thought about you all weekend."

At the use of my twin's name, I manage a wobbly smile. "Me too."

It's the truth; I did. I had such a great time with my sister's boyfriend, I actually lay in bed after that date, unable to sleep, seeing Dash's dark eyes every time I closed my eyes.

"Don't you want to see where this goes?"

Oh my God, he's asking if I want a relationship. He wants to date me—I mean, he wants to date Lucy.

This is my chance to break up with him. I won't have a better opportunity.

I swallow, gathering my courage.

"Date me exclusively?"

"*Sí.*" *Yes.* He laughs, my eyes drawn to his throat. "Figured I might as well bring it up now before we waste any more of our time."

Shit. He must really like my sister or he wouldn't have brought up the relationship talk before there was an actual relationship.

I've never met a guy like this before. Never.

And I'm not likely to again.

He tips his head back and laughs, the column of his thick, masculine throat contracting with the effort. I peel my eyes away, swallowing hard, squirming in the wooden chair.

God his throat is sexy.

"You want to talk about dating me? *Now?*"

I'm fascinated.

"Can you think of a better time?" His wide shoulders lift into a shrug. "I have no idea what normal guys do in these situations, but I think playing games is a waste of time. I also have no problem telling you what I want."

"Uh huh." I scan the perimeter, searching for the closest exit. A bathroom. A place where I can covertly text my sister.

He leans in farther, large body half across the table, only inches from my face. "*Te ves preciosa cuando estás nerviosa*, do you know that?"

He thinks I'm cute when I'm nervous?

"Am I?" I'm practically whispering.

"So fucking cute."

He is too sweet. "*Gracias.*"

Suddenly, breaking up with him feels terribly wrong; all I want right now is to get up from the table and climb into his big lap and kiss his gorgeous face. That beautiful nose.

Those full, sculpted lips.

What the hell is wrong with my sister?

What the hell is wrong with *me?*

I want him for myself, that's what's wrong with me! I might not believe in Insta-love or fairy tales or sparks flying when you first meet someone, but if I did, I'm adult enough to admit that I'm feeling them now.

That I felt them as soon as I laid eyes on him standing on my twin sister's porch.

"You need some time to think about it?"

"Huh?"

"About what you want to eat, and whether we're going to keep seeing each other. Be honest." He shrugs again. Shoots me a gorgeous, brilliant smile.

"Honest...right, for sure."

"Are you worried I won't have enough time for you?" He reaches across the table for my hand, but I pull mine back, resting it in my lap, where it's safe. "My friends fight with their girlfriends about that all the time. I'd say it's a huge problem for most of them. What are you afraid of, Lucy?"

For one, he can stop calling me Lucy. It's making my skin crawl, makes me feel guilty. Makes me jealous. Resentful.

Depressed.

What if I'd seen him at the party first? What if I was the type of girl who had the courage to ask someone like Dash Amado on a date? Would things be different? Would it be *me* he's looking at the way he's looking at Lucy?

Lucy.

She's not just my friend; she's my sister. We're blood, and she will always come first.

Always.

***

DANTE

Something isn't right with Lucy.

I can fucking feel it.

Since our date on Friday, nothing is making any freaking sense.

For one, she's wearing a goddamn turtleneck.

Why is this strange? Because her boobs are always on full display. She's one of those girls who's constantly at the baseball house, desperate for attention, letting it all hang out.

I'm a *guy*, one with a fully functioning set of eyes, and from what Lucy has shown me, she has a fantastic rack—which is why it's so fucking odd that tonight she's buried in black cotton up to her chin.

Tonight, her long hair seems longer, windblown and natural. Messy, like she rolled out of bed to come meet me and didn't spend an hour in the bathroom curling it.

Her perfume, which used to smell like pure gold digger, now has traces of citrus and flowers and vanilla, hitting my nose when she flips that mass of hair over her shoulder.

She looks different tonight, conservative.

She's barely wearing makeup, just some mascara.

And—obviously—the whole turtleneck thing is confusing as shit.

The black color is stark against her pale skin. That's another thing throwing me off—the few times I've been out with Lucy, her skin has been a warm hue of...well, *orange*.

This Lucy? She looks like someone I could actually bring home to *mi madre*.

I shoot a quick glance at the front of her sweater; it might be covering the entire column of her neck, but it's tight, outlining ample curves I don't remember her having. Large silver hoops catch the light from the modern chandelier above, her one vanity.

"We can talk more after dinner," I tell her.

Her chin tips, lips say, "Okay."

A tentative smile.

We're quiet while I look at the dinner selections and steal glances at her over my menu. Lucy is staring at hers, biting down on her bottom lip, undecided.

"Need help deciding?"

"I, uh, didn't realize they had food, so I wasn't prepared for dinner."

Annnnd *there* it is. I swear to God, if she's one of those girls who eats like a fucking bird—salad with no dressing and a side of water—I'm going to seriously reconsider dating her.

"Did you already eat?"

"No."

"Are you *hungry?*"

Her head lifts. Our eyes meet. "I didn't really come here to eat, but yeah, I am hungry."

My lip curls. "Let me guess, you're going to have a salad."

"Well, let me see." She lifts the menu and disappears from sight as the waitress approaches and glances between us.

"Are you all set to order, or do you need a few more minutes?"

Lucy reappears from over the giant folded menu. "I'm ready if you are."

"Ladies first."

"Okay." Her index finger trails along the first page's entrées. "Can I get the filet please, medium rare, with a wedge salad—ranch dressing—and a baked potato with sour cream? And bacon."

She closes the menu and hands it to the waitress, clasping her hands serenely. Lifts her brows my direction.

Damn, I'm impressed.

"I'll have the same." I hand my waitress the menu, mimic Lucy's pose. "So."

"So."

My head tilts and I relax into the hard back of the wooden chair. Across the table, my date does an inventory of me that has nothing to do with physical attraction; oddly, she hasn't flirted or giggled at me once, another thing that seems…off.

Her eyes scan my broad shoulders—the width earned through hours of busting my ass on the diamond—up my thick neck, landing on my lips. My high cheekbones, the left one with a stitch holding it closed. My expressionless eyes and tired brow.

Her lips part. "Where did the bruises come from?"

"Someone's bat."

"I thought catchers wore face masks!"

"We do."

Those blue eyes go wide. "Have you ever lost a tooth?"

"Yes." I tap on my teeth. "This front one is fake."

"On a scale of one to ten, how bad does it hurt to get jacked in the face with a baseball bat?"

That's an odd way for a girl to put it, but the answer is easy: "Fifteen."

"What are your plans after college?"

I pause.

We've already discussed this, on our first date when she peppered me with questions about my odds of playing professional ball, how soon that was going to be, and if I had an agent.

"The pros." I drag the words out in a *duh* tone of voice.

She cringes. "Oh yeah, right. Sorry, I forgot." But then, "But you have a major, right? What are you falling back on, just in case? What happens if you get hurt?"

No girl has ever asked me that. "If I don't get drafted, I'll…" I shift in my chair uncomfortably. Discussing what would happen if I weren't eligible for the draft isn't something I normally talk about, not with girls like Lucy, girls who have no real investment in my future other than a meal ticket. "DNR."

"Department of Natural Resources?"

I blink. "You actually know what that is?"

She shrugs. "My dad likes to fish."

"What about you?"

"What about me?"

"What are you doing when you graduate?"

"I've never told you my major? That is so unlike me."

Did she just admit she likes talking about herself? I chuckle.

"You've told me you're a fashion major, but never said what you plan on doing with your degree. We didn't exactly do a lot of chatting on our first few dates." I shoot her a lazy smile.

"Oh. Right." Again, she tucks those long locks of hair behind her ear, causing her earrings to shine in the light. "My major is, uh, fashion design."

Now she's repeating herself. "You told me that already."

"Right, sorry." She avoids my eyes, taking a drink, suddenly fascinated by the heavy burgundy draperies covering the walls. "So, Dash, what's your real name?"

"Don't you think you should know if we're going to give this thing a shot?"

Lucy cringes. "Yes?"

"The fact that you're asking means you haven't adequately done your research. Haven't you tried looking me up at all?"

"I haven't had time?"

"It's Dante."

"*Dante*," she repeats quietly to herself with Spanish enunciation. Bites back a smile. "Dante Amado," she says, articulating my entire name. "Huh."

"What about Lucy, that short for anything?"

"She's—*I'm*, uh, named after our grandmother—*my* grandmother." Her head shakes. "Lucille. Lucy is short for Lucille."

Lucille *does* sound like someone's *abuelita.* The name is unsexy and unfuckable.

We're interrupted by the busboy refilling our water glasses. "Thank you," she says with a smile.

I recognize the dude from my environmental law class and give him a nod. "Yeah, thanks."

For a few moments, we sit in silence, and I feel Lucy sneaking glances. Then, "If you could live in any city, which one would it be?"

This one is a no-brainer. "I'd play for the Rockies."

My date rolls her eyes. "That's not what I asked."

"It's not?"

"No. I asked if you could *live* in any city, which one would it be. I didn't ask where you would *play.*"

"Oh. Well…" I set down my fork. "*No lo sé.*" *I don't know.*

Lucy tilts her head and studies me, eyes softening. "That much of your future hinges on you getting drafted, huh?"

I raise my head, meeting her eyes. "Yeah."

Her clear gaze bores into me. "What's it like?"

"What's what like?"

"The *pressure.*"

For a second, I want to tell her that's a strange fucking statement to make, but then I go quiet and think about it, really sit and think.

She's right.

It is a lot of pressure, especially since *mi familia* is depending on me to make something of myself.

All the money my parents sank into a lifelong baseball career that isn't even an official *career* yet, that's nothing but a goddamn hobby if I don't get drafted.

No one but *mi mamá* has ever asked me how the pressure makes me feel.

And now Lucy.

This—*this right here* is why I found myself really fucking liking her last weekend on our date. I think she might actually give a shit.

"It's heavy."

I don't mind saying it, admitting with two words that I have a world of weight crushing down on my shoulders, broad as they may be. It feels...

Whatever.

It hardly matters; my life is mapped out for me, and there's no getting off the path I'm already treading on.

"So where would you want to live?" Lucy prods again, still wanting an answer. "If you could choose."

"I don't know. I'm never thought about it."

"Well I have—I love the Midwest. I love the change of seasons. I've always wanted to live where I could ski in the winter and enjoy the sun in the summer, you know?"

"You love the Midwest? Are you nuts?" I hate everything about it—the rain, the hot, muggy summers. The cold—every damn winter I come close to freezing my balls off.

"You just said you wanted to move to Colorado to play for the Rockies!"

I laugh. "For *work!*"

Lucy shrugs. "No take-backs."

The server chooses that moment to appear with our appetizer salads: two plates of fussy lettuce, one tomato, and two cucumbers each. Rabbit food. Irritated at the small portion, I poke at the plate with the tines of my fork.

A soft chuckle has my ears twitching.

"¿Qué es tan gracioso?" What's so funny? I want to know.

Another laugh. "You. You're pouting because the salad is so small."

"So?" I grunt, stabbing some lettuce with my fork and shoving it in my gullet—and just like that, half of it is gone.

"Are you mad because there's nothing on the plate?"

My answer is a scoff.

"How about I give you whatever I don't finish?"

This perks me up considerably. "Are you planning on not finishing the salad?"

"No, but I figured the offer would cheer you up."

It does.

I'm starving, ravenous, and her offer to let me finish her plate? Fucking adorable.

"Hey Lucy?"

"Hmm?"

"Know what I'm going to do?"

"What?"

"I'm going to date the shit out of you."

CHAPTER SEVEN

AMELIA

I'm going to date the shit out of you.

That is not good, and now my pits are sweating.

Dante isn't just eyeballing my salad like he hasn't eaten in days; he's staring at me the same way, like he's trying to figure out what's different about me all at the same time.

Lucy and I are night and day.

Most people still can't tell the difference, including our parents, so Dante's intensity is throwing me off like a curveball. It's unexpected in the best possible way.

No one has ever been able to tell us apart.

Dash is the opposite of everything I was expecting.

It's making me…

Jealous.

I'm jealous of my sister.

I knew he'd be handsome, but I didn't realize he'd be serious, or intuitive. He's direct and open, and the longer we sit here, the chattier he's becoming.

I like it.

I like him.

I'm attracted to him, too, which is *terrible*, because

Lucy, Lucy, Lucy.

Because I'm here to break up with him, not charm him into another date. Jesus, I'm so bad at this.

When the server brings our entrées, I feel Dante watching me, tracking the movements when I lift my knife. Cut a small piece of steak. Pop it in my mouth and chew.

I'm afraid to look him in the eye, so I stare at the wall behind him. The curtains. The older couple at the table behind us.

Cut another piece, take another bite.

It's hard work ignoring him.

He's big and intimidating and sexy.

His gray shirtsleeves are pushed up to his elbows, muscular forearms flexing when he cuts the meat on his plate.

"So what else do you do when you're not studying fashion?" he enquires. "What do you do for fun?"

I try to channel my sister; these answers are easy. "I like listening to music."

Oh God, that sounded so lame.

"Listening to music in your free time? What do you do, lie on the bed and stare up at the ceiling?"

A laugh escapes my lips. "Something like that. Um, let me think, what else do I like to do…"

Lucy likes: traveling. Shopping. Getting her nails done. Going for coffee with her sorority sisters.

It sounds so shallow, I'm embarrassed to let the words pass my lips. Shopping and nails and coffee? *Ugh.*

"I love the stars, and I do a lot of hiking."

Lucy is going to kill me.

First I slip and start speaking Spanish, and now I've gone and told him I love astronomy. Lucy hates it outside, hates the wind and cold weather and snow.

If Dante takes her into the woods, she will throw a conniption fit.

"You know that set of bluffs you can hike to? The one past Coleman Hall?" There's a road you can take that winds around a huge hill, up and up; once you reach a certain point, you can park your car and climb the rest of the way up to a scenic point that overlooks the entire city. "I like going up there when it's overcast."

Panoramic views so far, you can see into the next state.

"Hiking?"

I avoid his intense gaze by pushing a mushroom into the steak sauce on my plate then popping it into my mouth.

"Yes. I, uh, went out west for spring break last year to Idaho and hiked a bunch of trails. Really anywhere with a view." I love it that much.

"I was in Montana for spring break."

"Doing what?"

"Snowboarding." He pauses. "Do you..." His voice trails off in a question.

"I ski." Lucy and I both do, something our parents insisted we learn. It's something I love, but my twin would rather parade around the chalet in cute ski clothes, flirting with the ski patrol and instructors that periodically come through.

"Why does that surprise me?" he asks, sitting back to study me.

"I don't know. Why does it?"

He quirks a heavy brow. "You seem more like the chalet kind of girl."

Ding ding ding! He certainly has my twin pegged better than most.

"You really shouldn't judge me by my appearance, and I'll try to do the same."

"You haven't judged me by mine?"

I give my head a little shake. "Honestly? Yes. I might have, just a little bit?" I hold out my thumb and pointer finger to illustrate the teeny tiny bit I judged him.

Physical appearances are the way Lucy chooses all her boyfriends. She spends hours on her hair and makeup to go out on the weekends, spends free time at the mall when she's not in class.

"Is that so?"

"Just a little." *Change the subject.* "Besides baseball, what is it you do for fun? What are your hobbies?"

"I work out a lot."

I crinkle my nose. "That's your hobby? Working out?"

He narrows his dark eyes. "*Sí.*"

"Anything else? Do you like to read, or watch movies, or, I don't know…" I think for a moment. "Go to the county fair in the summer?"

His expression is as blank as his tone. "The county fair."

"Rides, games, cotton candy…"

"As a matter of fact"—the corner of his mouth curls—"I did go to the state fair this summer."

"Same. I'm freakishly good at the ring toss."

This information must surprise him because he laughs. "What else are you good at?"

He's purposely laying down the groundwork for an innuendo, but I ignore it. Best not to go down that path.

"Darts," I deadpan.

"Darts?"

"Yeah, like in a smoky bar. The more beer I've had, the better I am."

"I would pay to see that."

"It's a sight. It's like"—I wave around a fork with a chunk of steak on it—"my stupid human trick."

"Wanna show me? I'll take you to Mad Dog Jacks and we'll play darts."

Mad Dog Jacks used to be a biker bar, but for whatever reason, the college kids in town have decided it's the perfect hangout on the weekends. Part dive, part…well, the place is a complete shithole no matter which way you look at it.

Nervously, I push the hair behind my ears. "I-I'll have to check my calendar."

Dash regards me quietly, eyes smiling. "You do that."

Before I know it, we've been here another hour, long after our food has been cleared away—so long I've completely forgotten myself and what I'm supposed to be doing here, ignoring all my sister's texts—the ones blowing up my purse. It's been vibrating for the past forty-five minutes.

Dante pays the bill.

Pulls out my chair and holds out my jacket so I can slide in. Guides me outside, hand at the small of my back, fingers gliding up and down my spine.

It's dark when we arrive outside, awkward when we walk to my car. The click of my heeled black boots against the concrete the only sound in the entire parking lot.

"Thank you for dinner."

"You're welcome." When he comes at me, presumably for a goodnight hug or kiss or whatever, I put my hands out to stop him.

"Dante." I take a deep breath, lean against the driver's side of my car, and look up at him. "We should probably finish the discussion we started inside."

"Which one?"

Oh Jesus. He's going to make me say it. "The relationship one?"

"Okay." His arms cross. "What about it?"

I'm definitely doing a crap job impersonating my sister. She wouldn't be having a conversation with him in a half-empty parking lot; she'd be leaning into him and running her palms up and down his hard chest. Planting her lips on his, no doubt sticking her tongue down his throat. Sucking on his neck and—*oh my God*, what am I even saying?

"I don't know if…" I clear my throat. Peel my eyes of the column of his neck.

"You saying you want to take it slow?"

"No." I can barely shake my head. "That's not what I meant."

He waits me out, silently—which is the freaking worst. If he was acting like an asshole or being demanding or pushing me into talking, I would have no problem kicking him to the curb.

Unfortunately, he's not doing any of those things. Dante is patient and willing to listen.

It's horrible.

"Want to go downtown for a drink? This was fun."

"It was," I admit reluctantly, feeling guilty for enjoying my sister's date.

Dash moves closer with purpose, and I propel myself backward until my ass hits my car door, sending me into a slight panic—he's definitely going to try to kiss me.

The problem is, I want him to—want him to so bad my lips are tingling.

Everything on my body is humming.

"But I should probably go."

I don't *have* to go; I don't *want* to go.

I *should* go.

Because he is not my date. He's my sister's, and I'm here to break up with him. I turn my back, unlocking the car to busy myself. Hand on the handle, ready to pull it open.

"You don't have a few more seconds to say goodbye?"

And by *say goodbye*, I assume he means *make out*.

"Not really—I should have been home an hour ago, sorry. Homework is calling."

"Darts then? Saturday? We can make asses of ourselves and you can show me how freakishly good you are."

"I can't."

"What about another night?"

"That probably won't work either."

"What the hell is going on here, Lucy?"

"I can't do this anymore…with you. I'm not…" I take a deep breath, blurting out, "I want to see other people."

"*Okayyy*." He takes a step back, jamming his large hands into the pockets of his dark jeans, brown eyes scanning my face, searching. "Not that it matters, but why didn't you tell me sooner?"

"I tried."

"When?"

"Now?"

"You know, most people just do this shit over the phone. You could have saved yourself a lot of time by texting me."

"It's not my style."

"Really," he deadpans. "Breaking up with people over text isn't Lucy Ryan's style." Dante snorts sarcastically. "*¿Por qué me cuesta creerlo?*" *Why do I find that hard to believe?*

All in all, this breakup is going great, considering…if you don't factor in that I like the guy I'm breaking up with, he doesn't know my true identity, and once he finds out I lied, he's never going to want to speak to me again.

But at least he's not shouting. Or acting hostile. Or being a jerk.

"I was really starting to actually fucking like you."

"I'm sorry." My voice is small.

"Trust me," he scoffs. "I'll get over it."

It's not mean or rude, but it stings.

Hurts.

Still, he doesn't walk away as I climb into my car and buckle in. Doesn't walk away as I back out of the space, shooting him one more longing glance through the rear view mirror, tears threatening to blur my vision.

He stands in the parking lot, in the same spot my car was just parked in, watching me drive away.

Watching *Lucy* drive away.

He likes her.

Me.

I like him.

And I hate myself for it.

***

DASH

When Lucy pulls out of the parking lot, I do something I haven't done in ages.

Go on social media.

Log into Instagram.

Search: Lucy Ryan.

Scroll through her account. Scan the dumb pictures of her partying, hanging all over her friends. Frat parties. There are several of her at our house on Jock Row, another on what looks like a girls weekend. Starbucks cups. Photos of her nails. Other random stupid shit *sin sustancia. No substance.*

Then.

There, in living color, is a photo that has me seeing double. I do an actual double take, eyes practically bugging out of my fucking skull.

Holy. Shit. There are two of her—two of them.

Twins.

I fucking knew it. I knew something was off with her.

My fingers slide apart so the picture expands—the shot of them together, standing with their arms around each other's waist, long, tan legs playing peekaboo beneath flirty dresses. Under a flower-wrapped archway, there's no denying they're both beautiful, the caption reading *Aunt Victoria's wedding #RyansTieTheKnot*

The really fucked up part of this whole thing? I can tell exactly which one I've been spending time with lately, and it sure as hell wasn't Lucy Ryan.

It was the girl on the right.

Under the dim lights of Zin's parking lot, I study that picture, zooming in on that face. Her hair. Her eyes.

They're identical, but it's their expressions that give them away: Lucy's trying to be confident and cocky while her sister is gorgeous and easygoing, letting her twin hog the camera.

I zoom again.

There's that dimple I love so goddamn much—one of them has it, the other doesn't. Lucy's hair is lighter, layered around her face, and cut a few obvious inches shorter.

And their chests? I was right about the tits.

Her twin is beautiful. What was she doing pretending to be Lucy?

They're nothing alike; any moron with a modicum of sense could have figured it out eventually—it only took me two dates with her to distinguish the differences.

Except I'm not fucking dating her anymore.

She dumped me.

Which is such bullshit, because after our last date together, I envisioned myself getting serious with a girl like her, doing all sorts of fun, outdoorsy shit together in the off season. Hiking and skiing and snowboarding, whatever she wanted to do.

I'd chase her anywhere.

We had a connection I'd bet money she felt, too. I would stake my ball career on it.

I'm a planner—always have been—so once the wheels get turning, there's no stopping this train.

I close Instagram, immediately tapping my phone to make a phone call.

It only rings twice.

"Uh…hello?" The reluctance in her voice makes me want to laugh.

"Lucy?"

"Hey Dash. What's up?"

I waste no time throwing down. "Why did you send your twin sister to break up with me?"

There's a long, pregnant pause on the other end. "My what? What are you talking about?"

She sounds so bewildered and confused.

"Cut the bullshit, would you? I saw a picture of you two on Instagram."

Nervous laugh. "Oh, *that* sister! I was confused for a second."

"How are you confused—just how many sisters do you

have?"

"Um, just the one?"

"The one you had pretend to be you," I deadpan.

Lucy sighs like she's had this same conversation before, like the speech is rehearsed. "I'm sorry Dash, it just isn't working out between us. I'm already dating someone else new, so…" The sentence trails off, unfinished. I swear to God she's filing her nails and not even paying attention.

"Too chicken shit to break it off yourself?"

"Oh my God, admit it, you didn't like me that much either. Ugh, get over it."

"You're right—I didn't like you that much." *But I like your sister.*

She gasps, shocked by my bluntness. "Hey!"

"Don't act surprised—you're not my type either." I'm walking to my car now and climbing in, staring out the driver's side window while we talk. "That's not why I called, so relax."

"I'm not trying to be rude, but why are you calling? I *did* just break up with you and don't want you calling to harass me."

"Technically, you didn't break up with me."

"By proxy I did."

Is she always this fucking exhausting? *Jesus.* "Look, just tell me one thing: has your sister said anything about me?"

She's quiet a few seconds. "Like what?"

"Like…" I stare around the empty parking lot. "I don't know. After we went out, did she say anything about it?"

"Can you be more specific?" Lucy laughs, and I want to reach through the phone and strangle her. "I'm kidding, but also, no. She hasn't said anything specific—why would she? It would be breaking girl code for her to admit she had feelings for you."

The line goes quiet a second time, and then she sighs. "But if you're asking me if I got any twin vibes that she likes you, then yes. Between you and me, I think she does."

Hell yeah! I fist-pump the night air. "How do you know?"

"I know my sister, and she's been weird the past week—really defensive, short with me, and, well, I sense these things."

"Is that a genetic twin thing?"

"Yeah, except she doesn't have the gift. She doesn't feel things like I do."

Impatient, I keep this conversation moving along. "I'm going to assume you don't give a shit if I date her."

"If you can convince her to date you after I just did, you have my blessing." She laughs good-naturedly, and I remember the reason I agreed to go out with her in the first place. "I honestly do not give a shit."

"Thanks for the vote of confidence."

"All I'm saying is, my sister has a way stronger moral compass than I do. She's going to feel guilty—really guilty admitting she has feelings for you. She won't want to, you know, make me mad or whatever."

Oddly, that news makes me feel better; I don't want to date anyone who would backstab her own sister.

Lucy interrupts my musing. "Can I ask you something

though?"

"Shoot."

"How did you know it wasn't me?"

"¿Estás hablando en serio?" Are you being serious?

"Can you not do that? I have *no* idea what you just said."

"Which would have eventually given you away." I smirk. "The first thing I noticed, though? You don't have a dimple near your lip like she does."

"That's true. I don't." She's smiling now; I can hear it. "No one can tell us apart, you know."

"Seriously?" I can't keep the scoffing inflection out of my voice. "I find that hard to believe. I can list at least five things she does that you don't."

There's another long pause before she takes in a breath. "Wow. I can't believe it."

"Believe what?"

"Well…" She pauses for dramatic affect. "There's an urban legend among twins that if you find the person who can tell you apart, that's like meeting your soul mate."

"Uhhh, let's not go *that* far."

"I'm serious!" Her excitement is palpable. "You might be her *unicorn.*"

Getting called a unicorn is where I draw the line. "I'm hanging up now."

"Wait!" Now she sounds positively giddy. "Wait, don't hang up yet! I just want you to know that I won't make this awkward. You and I barely fooled around, and truly, it was like kissing my brother."

Awesome. Just what I wanted to hear. "Gee, thanks."

"For real. We had zero chemistry," she rambles on. "Like, *none*."

"The chemistry between you and me is nothing compared to what I have with your sister."

"*Ahhh.*"

"One more thing before I let you off the hook for pulling a twin switch on me—I'm going to need you to do me a solid."

"A solid? What's that?"

"You know, a favor?"

Pause. "Yeah, okay. Let's hear it."

CHAPTER EIGHT

AMELIA

L ucy: So how did it go tonight? Did you finish the job?

Me: Do you have to make it sound like I'm a mob hitman with a contract out on someone?

Lucy: Yes, because it sounds more exciting that way, don't you think? You know how I fancy the idea of being a mob princess.

Me: Tonight went well.

Lucy: WRONG ANSWER! That was a test, and you failed it. Do you know why?

Me: Um, no?

Lucy: Because Dash Amado just texted to see if I still want to play darts this weekend. DARTS, Amelia.

Lucy: Amelia, WHY WHY WHY is Dash texting me about another date? Let alone playing DARTS. You were supposed to DUMP HIM for me.

Me: I DID!!!! I did break up with him. I have no idea why he texted you, I swear.

Lucy: You must not have done that good of a job.

Me: Trust me, I did. When I drove off last night, the two of you were 100% broken up.

Me: I think?

Lucy: Don't do that.

Me: Do what?

Lucy: Don't punctuate it like it's a question. You were there—this shouldn't be a question.

Me: Yes, I'm sure I did. I broke up with him.

Lucy: Then why do I feel you hesitating?

Me: You really need to stop doing that. You are not telepathic.

Lucy: How do you know I haven't been blessed with the gift? Maybe I'm the twin gifted with that superpower, and it's finally getting powerful now that I've come of age.

Me: That is one of the dumbest things I've ever heard you say.

Lucy: But it's true.

Me: Fine. What's MY twin superpower?

Lucy: I don't know. You're good with small animals, being fake Lucy, and fake breaking up with boys?

Me: Haha, very funny.

Lucy: So just tell me this: if you for sure dumped his ass, why is he messaging me??

Me: Can you not say "dumped his ass"?

Lucy: Does it bother you when I say dump?

Me: Kind of.

Lucy: Why? Don't tell me you feel bad.

Lucy: How did the dumping go down?

Me: We were in the parking lot, talking, and I said dating him wasn't working out, and then I got in my car and he got in his car.

Lucy: Did you actually see him get in his car?

Me: No? Wait, why does that matter? The job was over so I drove away.

Lucy: You had ONE job Amelia, one. He wants to go out again, so…you tell me what we should do. I don't like him.

Me: STOP YELLING AT ME, and stop saying WE. He isn't my boyfriend.

Lucy: He wasn't mine either! And why are you freaking out?

Lucy: Amelia, tell me the truth—do you like him?

My fingers hover over the keys, thumbs frozen.

Me: I think he's nice.

Lucy: Nice, LOL. I bet he'd love hearing that. Nice is so boring. HE is boring.

Me: I don't think he's boring.

Lucy: That's because YOU'RE boring.

Me: Give me one more night to break up with him. I'll do a better job, I promise—although I'M POSITIVE I already did. He even said the words "breaking up". 100%

Lucy: Darts. Saturday night. 8:00

Me: Fine. I'll be there.

Lucy: Okay, but can I just say something? Darts are SO WEIRD.

CHAPTER NINE

AMELIA

Why did I agree to this?

I've broken up with this guy once already, in what were the worst five minutes of my life.

So why did I agree to meet him? Because I, Amelia Constance Ryan, am a glutton for punishment and cannot get Dante Amado out of my damn mind. Is it crazy that he's all I can think about?

I'm dying to see him.

He's got me longing for things I didn't know I wanted, and now I completely understand why my sister dates around.

It's been fun. And sexy. And a whirlwind.

Dante is great, and I like who I am when I'm with him.

It's true, we didn't spend that much time laughing, but to say there was no chemistry is a lie.

I was instantly attracted to someone my sister is dating and I hate it. I've never been jealous of her, but I'm jealous now, and I'm an idiot because I walked here, knowing he would be forced to drive me home at the end of this farce.

Does that make me a terrible human being?

Or just human?

He's easy to find when I walk in, hovering near the door, waiting—for me. Dante straightens to his full height when he sees me. I'm bundled up in my coat because it's insanely cold out, and he smiles at the sight of it.

He smiles at the sight of *me*.

I blush despite myself, beginning the process of unbuttoning the navy blue wool jacket, the toggles pulling free one by one.

It slides off like a robe, falls out of my hands and onto the floor.

Dash and I both bend to grab it at the same time but he beats me to it. We rise slowly, eyes connecting. Faces inches apart.

"Hi."

"Hi yourself."

"Thanks for meeting me here."

"Uh, sure." I tuck a stray strand of hair behind my ear, nervous about what to expect. "I didn't think I'd hear from you again after I broke up with you."

"Did you though?" His smile is pleasant, placating in an almost patronizing way.

"Are you trying to make me lose my mind? Because I remember our conversation *very* clearly, and we broke up, so I guess I'm confused about why you want to see me again."

Holy shit—what if he's some roid-rager, or a psycho who's going to start stalking my sister?

"I'm not trying to make you think you're losing your mind. I'm just questioning whether or not it was *you* that broke up with me."

I sigh. Some guys have such fragile egos. "I'm okay with you telling people you're the one who broke up with me. That's fine, however you wanna do it."

"You're totally missing my point." He winks, lips twisting into a grin—a smirk, really—eyes shining with mirth.

Something about the way he's observing me makes my stomach take a nosedive, and I actually lay my hand over my abdomen, pressing down to quell my nerves—to no avail.

Dante begins the short walk between us. Now he's standing directly in front of me, hands reaching to grasp my wrists, gently stroking with his thumbs. I glance down between our bodies, at our joined hands, then back up again.

"Dante, we broke up." I can barely choke out the words.

His dark gaze coolly assesses me. "Did we?"

He is going to make me insane.

Under the circumstances, I absolutely shouldn't be here tonight, shouldn't be seeing him again, the many reasons so numerous I can't resist tallying them up in my mind:

1. He was my sister's boyfriend
2. The boyfriend I broke up with for her
3. While pretending to be her
4. And ended up liking him
5. A lot
6. With a stupid amount of lust thrown in for good measure
7. He makes me crazy

8. I can't stop thinking about him

9. God, look at him staring at me

10. He was my sister's boyfriend

"I reserved us the dartboard in back but we're going to make this quick."

For real, he still wants to go through the motions of playing darts? Is this guy unhinged? I'm his ex-girlfriend!

"Uh, okay."

"You throw one and I'll throw one, then we can leave."

My eyes narrow doubtfully. "You brought me here to shoot one dart? Is this some kind of ploy to get back together? Because it's not going to work."

Dante busies himself by opening the container of darts, laying two on the table. "I have no intention of getting back together with Lucy."

I cross my arms, slightly irritated he's going through so much effort to win my sister back. "Do you do this with all your ex-girlfriends?"

"I don't have any." He laughs, picking up a dart from the table and handing it to me then grabbing one for himself. "And we both know you're not my ex-girlfriend."

"Uh, *okay...*"

He gestures for me to step up to throw. "Ladies first."

I'm so confused that I actually move forward without arguing, glancing back to study him before facing the board, the long heavy metal dart weighted in my fingers.

What the heck is going on?

Closing one eye to concentrate, I instinctively bite down on my tongue. The dart releases from trembling fingers, heading straight for the red outer double ring. Sticks in and hangs there proudly.

My hand is still shaking when I lower my hand, stepping off the duct tape on the floor so Dash can take his turn.

"Looks like someone isn't as calm and collected as they thought they were." His mouth isn't smiling but his eyes certainly are, palms rolling a black dart between them, eyeing the board shrewdly. He points the dart at me.

"If I get a bull's-eye with this, you spend the rest of the night with me, and I get to kiss you."

"Are you insane?"

He ignores my question, asking one of his own. "Do we have a deal?"

The odds of him actually hitting the target dead center, on the first try, without warming up, are slim, so I nod my head in acquiescence. Plus, if he makes the shot, I'll finally know what it's like to have those lips on mine, even if it's just once. I deserve it.

"Yes, we have a deal."

"Shake on it?"

I stare down at the large hand he extends, that calloused palm and the rough pads of his fingers. Glide my hand across his flesh, shivering when our skin connects.

It's positively electric.

We both shiver.

I give him a limp shake, eager to free myself from his grasp, tucking my hand away for safekeeping, the tingling sensation lingering far too long to be comfortable.

Far too long to be forgettable.

Dante steps in front of the dartboard, plucks my small silver arrow off, sets it aside, stands on the marker taped to the floor. Focuses on the target against the wall, homing in on that red, round center, leaning with one leg kicked behind him dramatically. His strong arm draws out the action of tossing the tiny missile.

My expressive eyes get wider when the dart lands the bull's-eye, heart damn near having palpitations when his heels pivot and he shrugs his shoulders as if to say, *Golly gee, look what I did!*

"Did you just hustle me?"

His shrug is easy. "Beginner's luck?"

"Liar."

Dante laughs. "You should talk."

We're staring at one another as if in a showdown, unwilling to bend.

This is getting awkward. "Maybe we should leave?"

"Thought you'd never ask. Can you hold on one second?" Removing his cell from the back pocket of his jeans, he taps open the camera. Positions it so I'm in the background of his selfie. Clicks.

"What are you doing?"

"Taking a picture so we can always remember this moment."

It's official: Dante is crazy.

He plucks his dart from the board, setting it in the box on the table. Grabs my jacket off the nearby chair then clasps my hand, tugging me through the crowded bar, past the throng, until we're shoving through the front door.

We stand under the fluorescent light on the side of the

brick building. It cast an unflattering, eerie glow.

I glance around, creeped out by the stark surroundings, wanting to leave, to go anywhere but here.

"Where should we go?"

Dante stuffs his hands into his pockets, shoulders slouching. "I hate asking you this, but would you mind coming back to my place? There won't be any distractions and we need to be alone."

"You want me to come to your place...to talk."

"Unless you're more comfortable at your place? I just think wherever we go, it needs to be just us." Dante shifts on his heels, shooting me a pointed look. "Don't you have shit you want to confess?"

Confess? Why is he putting it like that?

He thinks I'm my twin, my goofy, carefree sister, who by all accounts doesn't have a care in the world, who dates two, three guys at once, letting me do her dirty work for her.

Falling for her latest conquest is *not* my idea of a good time.

I'm a fool for standing here, a damn fool for coming.

"Let me get this straight: you want me to come back to your place even though I broke up with you? What are you, a glutton for punishment?" I let the sarcasm slip.

"I know I'm an idiot. I've done some really stupid shit in my life and chasing you just might top the list, but I like you, so yeah, I guess you could say I'm a glutton for punishment."

My nostrils flare, jealously flaring up. "You don't even *know* me."

"You're right, I don't." His head tilts to the side. "Whose fault is that?"

"What's that supposed to mean?"

"You've been *lying* to me—but guess what? I like you anyway."

My mouth gapes open, and I struggle for words. "I…"

We're under the glowing neon sign of Mad Dog Jacks, still standing under the bright, fluorescent light, arguing, it would seem.

"What would m-make you think I've been lying?"

"Let's not do this here." His shoulders rise and fall casually.

"Just say what you came here to say," I press. Then add, "Please," for good measure, practically begging.

His chin goes up. "What's your name?"

"M-My *what*?"

"*¿Cuál es tu nombre?*" What's your name?

My heart—*oh my God*, my heart is beating, thumping so wildly inside my chest I actually raise my arm, resting my hand upon it like I'm about to recite the Pledge of Allegiance. I press down, breathing heavily in and out…in and out, grasping to get control of my voice before I speak.

"Wh-What do you mean?" Playing dumb: one more thing Lucy and I have in common, although she's always been better at it than I am.

"You're such a terrible actress."

I say nothing; I couldn't possibly.

Dante's hands come out of his pockets so he can throw them in the air, frustration tangible, intense. "Would you just tell me! Tell me the truth. I've been really patient here, putting up with this twin bullshit." He blows out a puff of air, trying to remain calm. "I know you're pretending to be Lucy."

I *feel* my eyes go as wide as saucers.

"Anyone with half a fucking brain can tell you're not her, and I've been going out of my fucking mind." His hands gesture around his head like his brain is exploding as he continues his rant. "Trying to figure out what to fucking do about this—pardon my French—because Jesus, I can't stop thinking about you. It's driving me crazy that you won't even say your name. Can't you understand that?"

My head nods slowly.

"Can you please just be honest about who you are and put me out of my goddamn misery? I swear, I don't even give a shit that you lied." He pauses. "Well, I *do*, but I won't be a dick about it. I'll get over it. I've done nothing but dwell on this the past few days, so can you do me a favor and just be honest?"

My breath is coming as hard and fast as his stream of words, steam rising from my mouth against the freezing pre-winter air. The tip of my nose is cold too, and probably getting red as we stand out here, gawking at each other.

Those large hands of his get stuffed back into the pockets of his jeans, and he watches me expectantly. "Now it's your turn to say something."

"I don't know *what* to say."

"Let's start with this: do you even give the slightest shit about me?"

I will not cry, I will not cry, I will not cry.

"Yes." My shoulders sag. "Yes I care."

He's closer now, arms at his side. "*¿Cuál es tu nombre?*" *What's your name?*

"*Yo me llamo,*" I begin, voice cracking. "Amelia."

My name is Amelia.

"Amelia," he repeats back, my name a revelation. "It's nice to meet you."

"How…" I swallow hard. "How long have you known?"

He falters briefly, choosing his words. "I knew something wasn't right almost from the minute I saw you. There were a few things that stuck out that I couldn't make sense of, then you smiled and I saw this." He takes his finger and touches the spot below my lip, the one he wanted to touch while we danced at the concert, only this time when his finger presses into it, I'm able to enjoy it. "And your laugh is different."

It's true. My laugh *is* different, lower and less chipper, not as flamboyant or brash as Lucy's tends to be, mostly because she likes drawing attention to herself.

"I have no idea what to say. We didn't switch places to be malicious. I was trying to help my sister, and this is a first."

"What's a first?"

"We've never been busted."

"I didn't bring you here to bust you for lying. I brought you here because I like you. I told your sister on the phone that I—"

"Wait, you talked to my sister? She knows?"

"Of course she does. I had to make sure she wasn't going to be all fucking pissed when I pursued you."

"Pursue me?"

"I said I was going to date the shit out of you, remember?"

"Yes." *How could I forget?* "What did Lucy say when you talked to her?"

"She's the one who helped me get you here." He rakes a mammoth paw through his dark, silky hair. "After you broke up with me, I stood in that goddamn parking lot staring after you, wondering what the fuck had gone wrong, adding everything up in my head. A few things you'd said didn't make sense, so I went to Lucy's Instagram feed."

My nod of understanding is slow. "And found our pictures."

He nods as well. "Yeah. That's when I called her—from the parking lot, I might add—to see if she'd care if I wanted to date *you*, not her. She basically tripped over herself trying to unload me." He laughs. "She really does not like me."

"But you don't like her."

"Not at all—I like you."

Swoon!

Nothing this romantic has ever happened to me before, ever, never in my life, and I doubt it will again.

"I'm thinking we should get out of here. I'm freezing my ass off."

"I'd like that." I close the space between us, letting my hands brush up his chest. "You know what else I'd like? Kissing you."

He dips his head a few inches so our mouths are a

breath apart. "Is that so?"

"I feel like we've waited forever, don't you?"

"It's really only been a week, Amelia."

God it sounds so good hearing him say my name.

Mine.

"Only one of the best and worst weeks of my life."

"Sometimes the anticipation is the best part of playing the game, don't you think? The expectation, the tension leading up to the big play."

"Is that what you think this was? A game?" I'm trying to be flirtatious, but I don't think it's going very well; he scrunches up his nose.

"No. I don't think either of you were skilled enough to keep it going that long. You seriously suck at method acting." He grabs my hand, and I feel butterflies. He kisses my forehead.

Ugh.

"Come on, let's go."

I go, willingly.

***

"Your friends aren't going to think this is crazy, right?"

We're outside on the large front porch of the baseball house, about to go inside. Dante's left hand is poised to pull the screen door open, foot propped on the threshold, his right hand gripping mine.

I stop him from going in with a gentle tug, worrying my bottom lip.

"No, why would they?"

"You dated one sister, now you're dating the other," I explain. "You don't think your friends are going to have a problem with that?"

"*Mi cielo*, my friends aren't going to know the difference. They're a bunch of idiots."

I blush at the term of endearment. *My heaven.*

"Okay. I just don't want them to think I'm, you know… shady."

"No one is going to think you're shady." His laugh is deep, amused. "If anything, they'll think it's fucking awesome I dated twins."

I snort. "You're not Hugh Hefner—you didn't date us at the same time."

"But I *kind* of did." He turns to face me, stepping down off the stoop and pulling me into his body, hands sliding to my waist.

"But it's not like you *knew*."

I watch his mouth, engrossed by his lips. "My friends would still think I'm badass if I told them about it."

"They'd think you had a threesome." I roll my eyes. "Because most guys your age are perverts."

"I'm not."

"That's right—you haven't even tried to kiss me." My chin tilts up smugly in his direction, cocking my right brow.

"You didn't want me kissing you, remember? I've waited because I'm a nice fucking guy."

"I didn't want you kissing me because I *liked* you."

His head gives a perplexed shake. "That makes no

sense."

"I didn't want you kissing me as Lucy. I wanted you kissing me as *me*."

He moves to cup my face between his palms, stroking his thumbs up and down my cheeks, giving me the tingles. "You are seriously the fucking cutest."

"No, you are." I'm trying to pucker my mouth between his hands, but just end up with fish lips.

"We're not going to be one of those disgusting PDA couples, are we?"

"You're the one with your hands all over my face." His big, rough, perfect hands. "Are you going to kiss me?"

His face inches closer. "Do you want me to?"

"Yes," I whisper. "I've waited forever for you to put those giant paws on me."

I don't know what I expected to happen when our mouths finally connected, but this wasn't it.

It's so much better.

Charged.

The slow, deliberate probing from his delicious tongue is like a dream.

Wet.

Jesus, he tastes so good, so stupid good.

Impulsively I push against his chest, backing him up against the siding of the house with a gentle shove, rubbing up on him.

Dante's palms grip my ass, squeezing. Drag me onto his firm body, into his hard-on, running those fantastic catcher's mitts up and down my backside. Tense.

His lips are full. Hard.

Soft.

I could swallow him hole.

It's not enough, not nearly.

I'm so hot right now, and horny, and *God* I hate that word but it's so true. I want to rip my clothes off so he can touch my body, so I can touch his. We've done the three-date thing; I'm ready to take it to the next level.

This kiss is ruining me—I wonder what actually having sex with him will do.

When we finally tear ourselves apart, Dante blinks. Blinks again.

Mutters, "Let's get inside."

"All right," I say breathlessly, eagerness vibrating all my nerve cells. "If you don't think your roommates are going to judge me, I'll go inside."

"I really think it's adorable that you think they'd be able to tell the difference—really goddamn adorable." He plants another heated kiss on my lips, leaving me dazed and feeling cold when he pulls back to push open the front door. "Besides, most of these guys aren't with the same girl twice, so who the fuck are they to judge."

They're sitting around the house when we walk through the door, Dash tugging me in. We pause in the entry to the living room, and I give a short wave.

"Hi."

"Guys, you remember Amelia."

They're all openly staring, friendly and interested. Curious, like a group of toddlers would be.

One guy—a huge ballplayer sprawled in the center on the couch, remote control in his hands—looks me over from head to toe, then back again, wrinkling his forehead.

"I thought you said her name was Lucy."

I grin, responding before Dante can. "Nope. It's Amelia. You must be confusing me with someone else."

The guy looked sheepish. "Shit, sorry."

Dante's index finger tickles my palm as we move toward the hall. "Anyway, we'll be in my room. Don't bother us."

When we're in his bedroom with the door closed, he turns to me and says, "That little fib slipped right off your tongue, didn't it?"

"I've had a lot of practice." I grin, slipping off my shoes, already comfortable. "Mostly with family members and a few unsuspecting teachers in grade school."

"You didn't even bat an eye when you lied to his face. Please don't ever do that to me."

"I was just teasing him." I grab Dante's thick arm, squeezing. "Which would be impossible with you since you can tell us apart."

"Lucy said I'm your unicorn." He laughs, tossing his jacket on a chair.

This gives me pause. "She did?"

"Yup. I'm a motherfucking unicorn."

***

DASH

The differences are remarkable now that I know she's a completely different person; they stick out at me like red flags.

Obviously, there's the hair, and the dimple. Her brows are arched higher, eyes sharper. Amelia has an air about her that Lucy doesn't; she's deliberate and thoughtful.

Her lips? Incredible.

She sheds her jacket, sliding it down her arms, hanging it on the chair I have at the table functioning as my desk.

Truth? Now that I have her in my room, I'm not sure what to do with her.

She surveys the space, hands on her narrow hips, taking it all in. There isn't much to see, just a bed, table, chair, floor lamp. The bare minimum, not even a television.

Nothing to watch, nothing to see, no where to go but the bed.

Really it's just a beige box where I sleep, and now I seem to have acquired a girlfriend to go along with it.

I take a seat on the edge of my mattress, legs kicked apart, leaning back. Watch her preoccupying herself with my shit. The laptop on my desk and the sticky notes on my wall above it. The few books I have stacked on the table.

"This is nice, clean."

"I'm really boring." It sounds like an apology.

Amelia turns. Starts toward me, stepping in between my legs. "I don't think so."

My hands automatically slide to her waist like we've done it a million times, pulling her in for a hug. I bury my face in her flat abdomen, nuzzling her sweater.

Her deft flingers pluck tenderly at the black hair atop my head then trail down my neck, landing on my shoulders. Back and forth, fingertips kneading the muscles there.

It feels like heaven.

"I don't think you're boring at all."

I raise my head. "No?"

"*Te encuentro fascinante.*" *I find you fascinating.* "I love your big hands. They do incredible things, wouldn't you agree?"

My hands *are* fucking big. I flex them against her ass, skimming them down her denim-clad butt cheeks.

She goes on. "And you're kind."

Kind.

That's something no girl has ever called me, but I suppose it's true.

My nose finds it way between her breasts, and she laughs when I give her another nuzzle. I can't wait to see her tits, can't wait to get her naked.

"And you're as turned on as I am."

"*Sí.*" My arms encircle her, the tips of my fingers gripping her inner thighs from behind, thumb beginning to slowly massage the apex. "*Te encuentro sexy.*"

Amelia bites down on her lower lip. "Do you think we're moving too fast?"

I raise my head again. Her mouth is *right* fucking there. All I'd have to do is raise my face an inch...

"We haven't done anything."

Yet.

"No." Her lips brush mine with a moan when my fingers rub the delicate nub through her jeans. "But I want to, don't you?"

"*Sí*, but we can wait."

"I don't think I can." Her hips roll.

"Amelia," I enunciate with my accent. "I want you to know I'm all in. I'm not going to bail on you if we have sex right away."

"All in? Already, Dante, after two dates?"

"Three after tonight."

"I can live with that if you can." Her sexy voice wavers. "Do you, um, have, you know…condoms?"

"I live in a house full of baseball players—there are condoms everywhere."

"In your drawer?"

"No." *Shit.* "I'd have to go find one."

"Just in case, maybe?" She backs away. "I'm a planner, very organized."

My kind of girl.

"Be right back." Planting an electrically charged kiss on her mouth, I bolt off the bed. "Make yourself comfortable."

Shutting the door behind me, I riffle through three bathroom drawers and one cabinet before finding a brand new box of condoms, thanking Christ I didn't have to go to the living room and ask for one.

It's bad enough that I'm planning to get laid in a house full of my roommates.

I palm the bright pink box, giving my door a gentle knock before reentering. "It's me."

Nudge the door open.

Stop dead in my tracks.

Almost drop the box to the floor, almost hurl it across

the room.

"Amelia...holy shit."

She's lounging on my bed in just her lingerie, breasts spilling over the cups of her bra. The material is lacy, sheer, and black. I stare at her pale flesh.

Her shoulders rise and fall apologetically. "You said to get comfortable."

Getting naked isn't exactly what I had in mind, but I'd be an idiot to argue and *mi madre no creo un tonto. My mother didn't raise a fool.*

I'm already tearing the shirt off my body when she says, "You have a shirt for me to wear later? Because I'm thinking I might spend the night."

Unbutton my jeans, slip them down past my hips. Kick them off to the side.

She's leaning against the headboard, watching me undress. "I've never met a guy so eager to be tied down."

Tied down, tied to the bed—either way, I'd be happy.

"I was bred to be with one woman, *mi cielo.*"

Amelia moves first, scuttling toward me on her haunches, meeting me in the middle of the bed. "Is that so?"

She places the tip of her finger in the center of my chest, above my heart, dragging it down my body. Down my solid pecs. Down my rib cage. Over my abs, circling my belly button.

My dick is stiff when she reaches the waistband of my tight boxer briefs, hooking the material, snagging it away from my skin. I think I stop breathing when the nail of her finger brushes the head of my cock, a pleasant smile pasted on her lips, schooled expression neutral.

Neutral except for her eyes.

Those are gleaming.

Predatory.

Shining when she clasps my hard-on with all five fingers. Gently squeezes through the thin cotton of my underwear.

"I'd wondered about the size of this." Her voice is a low, seductive murmur. Her hand? Giving me another squeeze. "And now I know. Hmm, your breathing seems labored. Do you want me to stop? Let you catch your breath?"

I shake my head like a dope. Swallow hard, wanting so badly to jut my hips forward and thrust. Grip her hand so she'll tighten it around my throbbing dick.

"It's probably a good thing you're in such good shape." She releases me—*the tease*—running both palms up my abs. "I've never dated an athlete before." Plucks a nipple. "And your skin is so smooth—well, except for these goose bumps."

Still, I wait, not touching her, knowing I'll get rewarded for my patience.

"You know what I like about you Dante? Besides the fact that you're so smoking hot and look incredible with no clothes on? I love that you're so levelheaded, so composed."

Amelia moves closer on her knees until her lace-covered breasts brush my chest. "I've never found anyone so sexy or attractive in my entire life."

I don't know what's making me harder—how upfront she is about what she wants or the fact that she's not wearing clothes.

When our mouths collide, one hand slides down her spine to cup her tight little ass, the other braced behind her head. Our kissing sounds fill the air, sexy moans and lapping tongues. We're messy and hurried and when Amelia starts rubbing her pussy against my dick, our pelvises grinding, it's time to get completely naked.

She beats me to it—reaches behind her back, lips still suctioned to mine, unclasping her bra in one motion. Pulls the straps down her arms, discarding the delicate black fabric on the side of the bed. Grapples for my hands, placing them on her tits.

I've never really been a boob guy, but I've just been converted into one. They're full, heavy in my hands, my thumbs brushing over her dark areolas at the same time Amelia pushes down the waistband of my boxers.

"*Eres mío*," comes her husky murmur. "*Mío.*" *You're mine*.

We're whispering all sorts of sexy shit to each other in Spanish as our hands explore, limbs entwined, falling to the mattress. Amelia lazes beneath me, hair fanned out on my pillow, permitting me to explore, dreamily twirling my hair when I latch onto her nipple, sucking. Arches her back. Runs her nails down my scalp, my neck.

I rise above her, index finger idly trailing up her underwear, up the front, thumb pressing down in small, lazy circles.

Round and round and round on that little pink nub.

Her fists clench the quilt covering my bed.

"Don't," she gasps. "Or I'll come."

My finger hooks into her panties, pulling them aside, fingers stroking. "You want me to stop, *cariño*?"

"Yes. Jesus, just take off your underwear and get on top. I can't take it anymore."

"You like it on the bottom?" *Good to know.*

We're shoving down our underwear and in a group effort, I kick mine off, roll on a condom. Hover over Amelia, dragging the hard length of my cock along her thigh until we're both moaning with anticipation, both of us eager.

Willing.

Ready.

"S-Sometimes I do." Her eyes are closed, teeth biting down on her lower lip.

"I wonder something." I lean in, sucking on her earlobe as I whisper, "Do you *really* think you deserve a good fucking?"

Her eyes open, nostrils flare. "*Yes.*"

I let my dick nestle between her legs. "I can't believe you fucking dumped me."

Amelia's hands pull down on my ass, urging me inside. "You are not bringing that up right now."

I reach between us, clutching my erection, running the tip up and down her slit, making her moan. "Oh, but I am."

When she pouts, turning her head and presenting me with the pale length of her neck, I lean in, sucking. "You weren't even going to tell me, were you?"

"No."

"That's really naughty of you."

"It is." She nods. "So naughty."

"You probably don't deserve this." I let the head of my cock creep in the smallest fraction.

"But you do." Amelia's face is flushed, hips beginning a slow roll, arms above her head. She looks ready to pass out.

"I do, don't I?"

"*Yes*," she hisses, panting. "God you feel good. *Ohhhh* shit…"

So fucking good, in and out.

In and out.

Just the tip, just the motherfucking tip—not even an inch—is ecstasy.

When she moans—so loud my roommates in the other room undoubtedly heard—I press a finger to her lips. "Shhh."

Her tongue darts out and flicks my finger. No sound comes out of her lips when she mouths, "*Fuck. Me.*"

We both do a lot of pleading, panting, and praying to Jesus, God, and everyone else while I'm balls deep inside her, rocking back and forth, muscles clenched.

It's gasping, desperate, breathless fucking.

My hands slide beneath her ass when I come, unloading inside, nose buried in the crook of her neck.

Mi cielo.

My heaven.

The End

Want to see more of Dante and Ameila? Catch glimpses of them in Jock Row, the first book in the Jock Hard series, releasing late Spring, 2018.

The following is an unedited preview of JOCK ROW: Book One in the JOCK HARD series...

FIRST FRIDAY
SCARLETT

"No offence, but you look like shit."

My friend Tess flips her perfectly coifed hair, eyeing up my soft, sweater. It's more appropriate for a bonfire or cozy night at home then a party, and when she said I look terrible she didn't mean I look sick.

She hates my outfit.

"Thanks Tess."

"I'm just being honest. Don't you want me to be honest?"

No. Not really.

"I'm getting over a cold, Tess. I'm trying not to get sick again." I couch dramatically into the bend of my elbow for good measure. "I've already told you this five time."

My voice takes on a low croak and I pat myself on the back for how authentic it sounds.

I'm not changing my clothes.

Not tonight.

"Can you at least take the scarf off?"

I finger the gray, cable knit length around my neck, breathing in the merino wool that's the only thing keeping my neck warm. "My scarf? What's wrong with it?"

"Nothings *wrong* with it—but we're going to The

Row."

When she says The Row, her voice changes. Fills with wistfulness.

The Row: the off campus housing block where student athletes live and party. Similar to Greek Row, each sport has its own designated apartment or house, spanning a city block. They study together, play together, live together. Hell, they even *eat* together in a special cafeteria, with super special, healthy jock food.

And Tess wants to date one.

Wants to date a ballplayer, emphasis on *player*.

And these boys on The Row? They're a different breed of student body altogether.

These boys don't even compare to the kind of guys from back home I'm used to flirting with. These guys? Are practically men.

Bigger. Brawny. In peak physical condition—probably the best shape they'll ever be in their lives.

Cocky.

Quick.

I've seen them in action on the ball field; I know the team is good. They definitely *look* good.

Smell good.

How do I know? I got too close to one while rooting around for a beverage at the football house last week—when he leaned over to grab the beer tap with his long, lean fingers, I accidentally caught a whiff. Checked out his upper torso and muscular forearms in the process, like every other female in the room with a set of functioning eyes.

I love my friends to death—tolerate them because

our history goes back to middle school—but sometimes, they're shallow and calculated and, well—Cleat Chasers. I'm not embarrassed by it, but it does get exhausting hitting Jock Row every damn weekend. Why? They're all hoping to sink their blood red talons into some unsuspecting athlete, myself often in tow. Bringing up the rear.

I'm third, fourth and fifth wheeling it.

Tonight Tess is on the prowl for a ballplayer, one ballplayer specifically: Dante Amado, a catcher she "bumped into" him in an administration building once. Discovered that if she timed it right, she'd run into him coming out of history class.

I guess I can't fault her, the guy is dark, broody and damn good looking. Latino to boot.

"Let's silver lining this: if I'm wearing this bulky sweater, he's going to assume I'm your DUFF and won't look twice at me. See? No competition."

Her dark head tilts as she considers it, puckering her hot pink mouth. "True, he would." Her blue eyes—the color of Ocean breeze contact lenses—rake up and down my body for the second time. "You know, you're going to be too hot in that thing. It might be cold outside, but it's not going to be cold inside the house."

"I'll go out on the porch if I have to."

She narrows her artificially enhanced blue eyes, and I'm surprised she can blink with all the mascara caked on her lashes. "What about your cold?"

"The worst of it is over. Can we just go? I kind of want to get home a little early and read."

"You've turned into such a nerd since you got your own apartment."

I ignore her. "What's taking Cameron so long?"

"One of her hair extensions was loose. She's adding extra adhesive."

Of course she is.

Cameron—Tess's roommate—chooses that moment to come sashaying out of their bathroom, thumbing a long strand of platinum blonde hair, curls sprayed into submission, the rest of them lying in silky waves. Dark eyes, glossy lips, and too few clothes, our girl Cam is ready to hit the Row.

She halts when she see's me, pointing an accusatory finger at my boots. "You're not wearing that outfit. It's butt ugly."

I roll my eyes. "Save your breath—I'm playing chaperone tonight. It's my job to keep guys off your jocks." I chuckle at my own witty quip. "Get it? Cause we're going to the baseball house?"

Cameron ignores my quip, checking her phone. "Should we walk or call a car?"

"Car," Tess's heels click on the linoleum. "I can't walk far in these shoes."

***

This sweater was a terrible idea; why didn't anyone stop me from wearing it?

It's so freaking hot in here; the first thing I have to do is lose this scarf.

Tugging at the end of it with my left hand, I pull it loose, lifting it over my head, loosening the round loop. Stuff it in my purse, which is more of a cumbersome tote, all the while holding a red cup in my right. It's red beer cup—except there's no beer in it tonight.

Just water disguised as alcohol.

And finding something to drink that isn't beer? Damn near impossible. I'd had to leave Tess and Cam to their own devices to scavenge the kitchen, raiding the fridge.

Surprisingly, I found an entire shelf of just water and juice. Snagged two bottles, one for now and one for later if I get thirsty, stuffing them in my bag. The last thing I need is a guy who lives here guys catching me ransacking their food supply and getting the wrong idea.

But they didn't have water at the makeshift bar (two sawhorses and a plywood board painted with the universities baseball logo and the rules for playing beer pong), so I did what I had to do to stay hydrated without getting wasted.

Stole two bottles of water.

My friends have already gone astray in the short time it's taken me to unwind my scarf, cooling myself by pulling at the front of my wool sweater, airing out, and taking a few refreshing sips of my pilfered beverage.

Delicious.

I fan myself idly, standing off to the side, surveying the room, trying not to die from heat stroke. A dramatic observation, sure, but if I manage not to pass out it will be a damn miracle. I'll never admit it, but Tess and Cameron were right—I shouldn't have worn this. Damn them.

Speaking of which…

I locate them near the front windows, my soft sweater suddenly *itchy*. Scorching. Making me sweaty and irritable and *oh my god why am I wearing this*? I slide a finger in the collar in an attempt to alleviate the temperature, giving yet another tug.

It's no use—I'm stuck sweltering in this godforsaken potato sack until we leave—and no way am I going out on the porch for fresh air alone.

I'm not brave enough. at this late hour.

But I'm brave enough to cross the room and join Tess and Cam, who are having better luck tonight than I connecting with people, already cloistered in a group with two of the more handsome young men I've ever seen.

Guh! I'm so awkward.

I approach quietly, sidling up in time to hear one of the guys say:

"...there's something wrong with my phone. Would you take a look at it?" He holds the jet black cell toward my friend, who eyes it with a goofy grin on her face, the little flirt.

"What's wrong with it?" she asks.

I step forward and finish the punch line he is about to deliver. "Your name isn't in it."

"Huh?" Tess wrinkles her brow, confused.

"The line is: there's something wrong with my phone because your name isn't in it." I pause. "Get it? I read it online somewhere, some list about best pick up lines. Or worst? I can't remember." I look up at into a set of scowling, brown eyes. "Did I get it right?"

"Oh! Ha ha!" Tess fake laughs, tapping him on the bicep, her fingertips lingering there. "You want my number? How sweet!" She takes the phone out of his hands, tapping her number into the contacts as he shoots a wary glance in my direction.

I clutch my cup, offering up a friendly smile. "Hi. I'm Scarlett."

He nods, but his mouth remains impassive. Quiet.

Is he pissed because I beat him to the punchline of his corny, pilfered pick up line? It's not even original!

"You should run and get yourself another beer," he pretends to peer into my cup. "Looks like yours is half empty."

I narrow my eyes. "Are you trying to get rid of me?"

"Me?" He manages to look affronted. "No! I live here. It's kind of my job to make sure everyone is having a good time."

"I'm good, thanks." I stare down into my cup. "Besides, this isn't beer. It's water and it's still pretty cold."

"Water?"

I scrunch up my nose. "Yeah—I'm not really much of a drinker, and I'm kind of sick, so—is it really a smart idea to get drunk?" I snort. "I don't think so."

His face contorts. "Where'd you find water around here?"

For real? "Uh. The kitchen?"

"Where in the kitchen?"

Is this a trick question? "Uh...the fridge?"

His eyes narrow. "We keep the fridge locked during parties."

My brows rise into my hairline. "You do?"

"Yeah. So no one takes shit." *Like water.*

My cheeks are on fire. I'm burning up in this damn sweater, and now totally embarrassed he thinks I stole—

purposely –taking shit from the house refrigerator.

Which I did.

But not on purpose.

Ugh! It was on purpose but completely accidental.

Crap.

"I'm sorry," I apologize. "I didn't see the lock on it. It opened right up."

He glances down his nose at me for the second time tonight, silently judging me. "Want something other than water? Maybe it will loosen you up."

Loosen me up? Is he serious?"

"You seem uptight," he continues, raising my dander.

I'd laugh if he wasn't so ridiculous. *Me?* Uptight? Ha! I'm one of the most outgoing people I know for heaven's sake! Just ask me!

"Thanks, but I'm good." I pull at my sweater, peeling it away from my skin. The room only seems to get hotter by the second. "So what were you talking about before I walked up?"

Cameron pipes up, resting her hand on the meaty guys bicep. "Benjamin was just telling us about how when the baseball team won the College World Series last year, it was because Derek pitched a no-hitter in the seventh inning."

Won the College World series? My brows furrow, the bridge of my nose pinched. "No he didn't."

"Yes he did!" She laughs. "He's amazing, Scarlett, you should hear the story." She pokes him. "Tell her the story Ben."

I look at Ben. Glance at Derek. Back at my roommate and shake my head. *These guys are full of shit.*

My mouth opens and more words come out that make the guy frown.

"USC won the College World Series last year. They win it almost every year." My water tastes warm when I take a drag, tepid at best going down my throat.

"How would you know?" Ben—the blonde Adonis—asks.

"My brother. He's obsessed with going to USC and playing ball there. He loves that school; it's so annoying sometimes," I tap my chin with a forefinger. "But I do remember last summer having to watch that dumb game—no offence—an entire week in June. The College World series is in June, right?"

The other blonde nods, crossing his arms and spreading his legs.

Now he's annoyed with me, too.

Great.

"Anyway," I prattle in an attempt to redeem myself. "I just remember being home and my brother watching that game every night after school. USC won, I'm sure of it."

Neither of the guys have a response.

Cameron on the other hand? Glares at them both. "Why would you say you won?"

"I must have been thinking of the year before," one of them lies.

"USC." I mutter into my cup, coughing. Both guys shoot daggers at me. "What! They did! Besides, you don't have to try so hard with these two. Try being honest with girls, it'll get you far."

I give them some encouraging advice and a smile, but neither are interested in being friendly. Not with me, anyway.

No. They want me to disappear.

"Aren't you sweating your ass off in that ugly sweatshirt?"

I glance down at the gray mohair confection. "It's a sweater."

"Whatever. Aren't you fucking hot?"

"Kind of," I admit.

"You should go outside and get some fresh air."

Yeah, that would feel great—but I'd rather not leave my friends unattended. Lord knows where they would disappear to.

The blonde, Ben, casually arches a brow and the guys exchange glances, so damn shady. I watch as he casually slides out of the conversation and disappears into the crowd, causing Cameron's bottom lip to pout. Arms to cross. Boobs to rise above the low neckline of her shirt.

I narrow my eyes, giving the remaining player a look. Are they trying to get rid of me?

"What did you say your name was?" Derek asks.

"I didn't."

His face is blank; impassive. Stony. And directed at me. "What's your name?"

"Scarlett."

His mouth curves. "Sober Scarlett."

"So you're a rhymer? Cheers." I hold up my red plastic cup, raising it in a toast. "Got any other set of skills?"

"You wouldn't know what to do with my other set of skills." He's pleased with his innuendo, which sends Tess into a giggle fit.

Gross Tess, no.

Just…no.

God, what is it with these guys? Are they all like this?

And why do my friends think they're so damn charming? They are the furthest thing from it. Crude. Sarcastic. I can tell by the cold glint in this one's eye that he's a colossal asshole.

Stereotypical D1 student athlete.

What a shame.

What a waste of a hottie.

What a dick.

Derek's face goes from a scowl to a smirk. "Heads up Sober Scarlett, the cavalry has arrived."

Huh?

Cavalry? He must be drunk.

The music goes from barely audible to an earsplitting decibel, so loud I can no longer hear what anyone is saying. Suddenly, I can hear nothing but moving lips and—

A large hand covers my eight shoulder, the weight of it warming my upper bicep, hotter than it already is. My head swerves, eyes settling on that large hand. Rough. Manly. Square tipped fingers. Short nails.

My green eyes travel upward, lifting their way up a tan, bare forearm, meeting a dark set of eyes; strong nose.

Full lips.

The human attached to that big hand is striking; not in a beautiful way—I wouldn't call him that. I wouldn't call him hot, or handsome, either.

He's way too intense for that.

Way too broody.

His eyes are a sullen brown, crinkled at the corner. Lips set in a straight unhappy line, just like his friends before him.

What is it with these guys? Why are they all so grumpy?

I feel my eyes widen when he leans his torso, warm breath brushing my ear. Leans down, into me, broad shoulders dipping and brushing against mine as that exquisite mouth speaks slowly near my ear.

I inhale, of course I do—he smells so good I can't stop myself.

"Can you follow me for a second?"

I shiver.

"Where to?" My eyes stray to the front door. The staircase leading to the second floor. The kitchen where I filched the water inside my cup.

"Over by the front door, no big deal. Just for a second so it's easier to talk."

Silent warning bells go off inside my head; this guy came out of thin air and suddenly has something to say to me in by the front door?

Isn't that weird?

What's the harm in following him to the corner? It's not like he's taking me to one of the *bed*rooms. It's not like he can try anything in a room full of people, right?

Right.

My eyes slide to Derek. To Ben, who has materialized. To Cameron and Tess, ogling me expectantly, both their manicured brows raised, stunned. I've seen these looks before; they're *excited*.

"Okay," I agree slowly. "I guess that would be alright."

"Follow me then, yeah? Stay close."

I nod, giving my friends one last sidelong glance before complying.

Whoever this guy is, his presence parts the crowd like the Red Sea as we wade through it, people clearing the way so he can get by.

I follow, gaze trained on his broad back. His broad, sexy back, muscles beneath his t-shirt straining with every step--every motion—the lines of his neck are tan and dense.

Tense.

His rich brown hair must have been cut recently, the lines precise. Short in the back, longer at the top of his head.

He shoots me a glance over his shoulder to make sure I'm still behind him before yanking the handle on the front door, then pushing the screen open.

I hesitate before following him onto the porch, foot poised on the threshold, cool air hitting me like a wall. I breath a sigh relief. Oh my god it feels so good; I was about to die in that hot, sweaty room.

In this stupidly thick sweater.

I step down onto the porch, over cautious, taking note

of witnesses in and around the yard. One, two, five people loitering on the lawn. Three on the opposite side of the porch. Two on the sidewalk near the road, smoking next to a car.

He appears to be doing the same; scanning the yard, doing a mental head count, nodding with satisfaction when he finally turns to face me.

Nonetheless, we both startle when the door slams shut behind us and we're alone on the porch.

He is tall—really *good and tall*—legs spread slightly, arms crossed. Typical baseball player stance, except no uniform. No glove.

"So. What's up?"

His nose dips down, studying me, those brawny arms uncrossing, the cords in his forearms stretching. "So. I hate to be the one to tell you this but you can't go back in the house

I laugh, rolling my eyes at the overhang above us. "Oh, oh-kay."

"I'm not fucking around right now. You can't go back inside—you're being kicked out.

I snort. "Who are you?"

"I'm the unlucky bastard that drew the short straw."

My nose crinkles. "What's that supposed to mean?"

"It means you're driving my friends fucking nuts and they don't want you back inside."

His mouth curves into a wry, patronizing smile. "And I drew the short straw for the honors to kick you out."

Wait. Is he being serious? "For real?"

"Yeah—like, for realz." He imitates an airheaded girl, fake twirling an invisible lock of long hair.

Except I'm not an airhead, I'm not stupid, and I'm not a—

"Cockblocker."

"I'm sorry, *what?*" I had to have misunderstood him.

"Inside they're calling you cockblocker. Because you won't stop running your mouth."

"I wasn't running my mouth!"

Without warning, he plucks the red plastic cup from my hand, sniffing the contents with that big, Greek nose of his. "What's in here, vodka?"

He sniffs at my cup again, taking a good, long whiff, sticking his nose inside.

"No," I contend indignantly. "That's not vodka! It's water!"

"Water? Where'd you get water around here?"

Not this again...

I hold up my hand to pause the conversation. "Hold up. Rewind: they're calling me Cock Blocker?"

"You're messing with their game."

I snort. "Your friends have no game. Unless you count *lying*, which isn't impressing anybody."

"What were they lying about?"

"Does it matter at this point?"

"Not really—they want you out and it's their house." But now he's curious, I can see it in his eyes. By the set of his arched brows.

"Look," I huff. "It's not my fault your friends are claiming they won the College World Series last year when they *didn't*. All I did was call them out on it—it's stupid that they're even lying about it."

"How are you so sure we didn't win the CWS?"

"Dude, seriously? You too?"

He laughs at my use of the word *dude*, Adam's Apple bobbing. "No, not me too. I'm not a fucking liar, I'm just wondering how you knew they were full of shit."

I shrug. "I have a baseball obsessed brother." I don't mention that Shaun is autistic and knows statistics about most collegiate teams, dating back before this guy was even born.

"Sucks to be you, I guess." His eyes stray to a window, gazing inside, longing to be back inside. "Look, can you leave? It's cold and I'd rather be back inside."

"You're seriously kicking me out."

His nod is authoritative. "Yup. This is me, officially kicking your scrawny ass out."

I do not have a scrawny ass! "That is the dumbest thing I've ever heard."

"Sorry ma'am. Can't let you back inside, you're disturbing the peace. I've been tasked with escorting you from the premises."

My head tips back again, and a nervous, giddy laugh— usually reserved for moments when I don't know how to react— erupts. Moments like *this* one that have me laughing like an idiot.

"Escort me from the premises? What are you, an undercover cop?" I sass, trying to turn my humiliation into a joke.

Only—if this is a joke, it isn't funny, not at all. It's embarrassing and awkward and now that we're out here on the porch in the cold.

"Can I at least go back inside and tell my friends I've been kicked out?"

"Nope." He obnoxiously pops the P. "I'm under strict orders not to let you back in."

"*Whose* strict orders?"

"Mine." One mammoth paw scratches across his stupidly sexy square jaw. "Come to think of it, I guess I am kind of like an undercover cop." His smile widens. "Yeah. I like that."

He smirks and *god* is he cute. So cute I have to glance into the yard to stop myself from staring directly at his white smile, chiseled jaw and sparkling eyes.

Jerk.

"Please let me go back in and tell them I'm leaving?" Jeez, now I'm begging. "Please?"

"Hell no."My arms cross definitely. "Text them if you want to let them know you're not going back in, they'll get it."

In a last, desperate attempt to gain footing, I stomp my foot like child. "I'm not leaving this porch until you let me back in."

He yawns, sounding bored. "Why are you being so dramatic?"

"Because! This goes against my…" I search for a word. "Civil rights!"

"Your Civil Rights," he deadpans dryly. "Do tell."

"You can't kick me out!"

"You're cockblocking my friends!"

"Your friends are pigs."

"You don't know that for a fact. Derek and Ben are fine lads."

"Fine liars, you mean."

"That too," he laughs.

"I'm not standing out on this porch while my girl-friends are inside. I'm not *abandoning* them." Although to be honest, I can guarantee they won't care that I'm not going back inside. We're friends, but we're not best friends, and our intentions for going out couldn't be more different.

"Sweetheart, if you don't leave this property, I'm going to end up babysitting you and that's not how I want to kill time on a Friday night."

My chin tips up definitely. "You punish me, I punish you. Seems like a fair trade."

His teeth rake over his bottom lip as he watches me, back and forth, gleaming white.

"Fine," he says at least. "While you're standing here being stubborn, I'll be over on the stairs."

Removing his cell from the back pocket of his jeans, he holds it up, thumb sliding across the screen, the glow illuminating his stupidly attractive face. He twists his wrist in my direction. "Do continue ranting. Don't let me stop you."

I eyeball him again as he settles onto a wooden porch step, legs spread out in front of him.

"You're really not going to let me back in?"

"Nooo." He drags the word out. "I'm *really* not letting you back in."

"What if I promise to zip my lips?" I run two pinched fingers across my mouth; throw away the key.

"Cute." His eyes are fastened to his phone. "But no."

"I can't be out here and leave my poor friends alone with those idiots." I pause. "Oops. Did I say the word *idiots* out loud? Take pity on me, please."

His head gives a slow shake. Tsks. "It's going to be a *really* long night if you keep doing that."

"Doing what?"

"*Begging* to get back inside."

"I'm not begging. I'm *asking*."

His eyes leave the screen of his phone, raking my person up and down with a dismissive brow. "It's begging—I know what the difference is and it's annoying."

The skin on my neck feels hot; the telltale signs of a blush brightening my face, even in the cold. "If...if you don't let me back inside, I'm calling the cops!"

"Be my guest." He takes a loud, slurping sip of his beer. "Tell them Rowdy sent you."

"You're impossible."

"Trust me, doll face, I've been called worse."

"Oh god—don't call me doll face."

"What should I call you then? I know you don't like the name Cock Blocker."

I stomp my foot, frustrated. "Ugh! Why do you have to be so stubborn?"

"You're calling *me* stubborn? Uh, *okay*." He mumbles

the word *Jesus* under his breath, and it's on the tip of my tongue to lecture him for using the Lords name in vain, but I bite the words back instead. For once.

"I-I...I'm sorry. I just..." feel helpless out here on the porch.

His eyes narrow as he studies me. "Bet you were one of those girls in high school that used to raise your hand during class to ask for extra credit."

My, "So?" slips out before I can stop it. What's wrong with raising your hand and asking for extra credit? That's how you get good grades and get ahead in life—going the extra mile.

"So. No one liked those girls."

I flush again, loosing count of how many times I've turned bright red in the amount of time we're been sequestered to the front porch. Alone, if you don't count the drunks loitering around the property.

I fake a scoff. "And you were one of those jockstraps that barely passed their classes and cheated off girls like *me*."

He spreads his arms, wing-span wide. "Yet here I am with a full ride to college. Imagine those odds."

I try another strategy. "What am I supposed to do until my friends come back outside?"

His head dips, and he's back to ignoring me in favor of his cell phone. "Not my problem."

"But they could be inside for hours!" Holy crap, where did that whiney voice come from? I really sound annoying.

"Want me to walk you home?"

"I'm not going home—and I'm not going anywhere

alone with you, but nice try."

"Really, you're not gonna to leave? Your friends had no problem ignoring the fact I hauled you off."

"Don't flatter yourself, you didn't haul me off. I followed you." Like a moron, because he was intriguing and cute and I was curious.

Curiosity killed the cat, Scarlett.

"Stay if you want, suit yourself." He eyes me up and down. "You're certainly dressed for it."

Was that a dig? I narrow my eyes, confident that it was a knock against my sweater. "I was sick last week! I had a cold!"

He holds up his bear paws. "Hey, no judgments. I'm just saying you're wearing a sweater that could double as a parka. I'm the one who's going to freeze their balls off in this tee shirt if it gets any colder."

"If you want to run in and grab something warmer, I can come with you." I smile sweetly. "Promise I won't disappear on you."

His lips twitch. "I think I'll take my chances against the hypothermia and frost bite setting in." He taps away at the lit up screen of his phone, the glow casting illuminating the bottom of his chin and nose. "Why do you think," he asks absentmindedly, "it bugs you so damn bad that your friends are getting hit on, but you're not."

"Is that what you guys thought I was doing? Being spiteful?"

His wide shoulders shrug. "Seems like it."

My mouth drops open, horrified. "I was not cockblocking my friends because I'm jealous!"

"So you admit it; you were cockbocking."

"No! That's not what I meant! That's not what I was doing; it's not my fault your friends lie."

"Is it because you're completely sober?"

"I'm not *completely* sober!"

"So are you *drunk*?"

"No! Of course not." I flip my hair, affronted. Seriously, the nerve of this guy! "I've been drinking water most of the night." Someone has to be the responsible and keep their wits about them.

Besides, if I was drunk I would have ripped this sweater off hours ago, but he doesn't need to know that.

"Let me get you a beer. Maybe your problem is that you need to take the edge off."

"Thank, but my only problem is that I'm out here, with you, and not inside where I'm supposed to be."

I'm fun goddammit!

"Fine, suit yourself," he grits out through perfectly white, perfectly straight teeth. Ugh. So good-looking and getting cuter by the minute, damn him. "Maybe you won't be so goddamn uptight while waiting for your friends and it will be more pleasant for both of us, yeah?"

"Uptight?"

"Yeah you're uptight." He squints over, shielding his eyes against the porch light. "Hasn't anyone told you that before?"

I stand my ground, answering his question with a question. "Why would make you say I'm uptight? Based on what?"

"Let me count the ways." He taps on the fingers of his right hand with his left. "I'm on this porch when I could be partying because you won't stop cock blocking everyone inside. You're wearing a fucking bear skin rug to a party. You're drinking water. You admitted to asking for extra credit during class. You won't stop arguing." Holds up his hand, wiggling his five fingers. "All signs? Point to uptight."

"First of all," I muster up a deep breath. "Those assholes didn't even give me a chance to *redeem* myself before they sent over their henchman. You."

"And second of all?" He smiles coyly, the cheeky bastard, leaning his heads against the newel post.

"Second of all, your friends were lame and not all at funny. They're lucky they're athletes, because if not, they'd probably never get laid."

The guy snorts. "Somehow I seriously doubt that."

I continue ranting. "Their conversation would have bored me to tears—so bloody mind-numbingly dull." I pause. "Can you imagine what they'd be like in the—"

I clamp my lips shut; I should not be discussing *sex* with this guy.

I don't even know him.

He is enemy number one tonight.

And he wants me to finish my sentence, of course he does.

"Can you imagine what they'd be like in theee...." He prompts me, unfolding himself from the steps, rising to his full height. Brushes off his jeans.

"I'm not discussing sex with you."

His grin almost makes me smile back. "I can fill in the blanks just fine all by myself, I'm a big boy."

He is a big boy. Larger than life, and for the first time since stepping out onto this porch, I wonder what his name is. Where he's from. If we've ever crossed paths on campus.

He stands over me now by a good foot, his lean hips resting against the white railing of the baseball house. Dark brown hair cut short. Tan skin. Beautiful full lips. His arms...

My eyes settle on those arms; settle on his wide shoulders and muscular deltoids. The bulge of his biceps and pec muscles. If he notices me checking him out, he doesn't mention it, instead, doing a brisk assessment of his own, beginning at my brown half boots. Up my black leggings. Over my thick, chunky sweater.

Flicker on my breasts, pausing.

I feel his eyes land on my lips, nose and hair. My long chestnut hair is pulled back into a tight ponytail almost at the top of my head, conservatively.

Boring, I suppose some would say.

I'm barely wearing any makeup; another bone of contention I'd had with my friends before leaving their apartment. Still, my skin is clear—this month during my period, I was spared an angry outbreak of the acne I normally would get.

Thank god.

My cheeks get hot as he stares—I feel my chest getting blotchy too, though he couldn't possibly see it.

OTHER TITLES BY SARA

For a complete updated list visit:

www.authorsaraney.com/books

ABOUT SARA

Sara Ney is the USA Today Bestselling Author of the How to Date a Douchebag series, and is best known for her sexy, laugh-out-loud New Adult romances. Among her favorite vices, she includes: iced latte's, historical architecture and well-placed sarcasm. She lives colorfully, collects vintage books, art, loves flea markets, and fancies herself British.

For more information about Sara Ney and her books, visit:

Facebook
www.facebook.com/saraneyauthor

Twitter
www.twitter.com/saraney

Website
www.authorsaraney.com

Instagram
www.instagram.com/saraneyauthor

Books + Main
bookandmainbites.com/users/38

Subscribe to Sara's Newsletter
www.subscribepage.com/saraney

Facebook Reader Group: Ney's Little Liars
www.facebook.com/groups/1065756456778840/

Made in the USA
Middletown, DE
11 August 2018